Is the

Bitch

Dead, or What?

☆ ★ ☆

*Also by Wendy Williams
and Karen Hunter*

DRAMA IS HER MIDDLE NAME

THE WENDY WILLIAMS EXPERIENCE

WENDY'S GOT THE HEAT

Is the *Bitch* Dead, or What?

WENDY WILLIAMS

and

KAREN HUNTER

THE RITZ HARPER CHRONICLES, VOL. 2

★ ☆ ★ ☆ ★ ☆ ★ ☆

BROADWAY BOOKS

NEW YORK

PRINTED IN THE UNITED STATES OF AMERICA

BROADWAY BOOKS and its logo, a letter B bisected on the diagonal, are
trademarks of Random House, Inc.

This book is a work of fiction. Names, characters, businesses, organizations, places,
events, and incidents either are the product of the author's imagination or are used
fictitiously. Any resemblance to actual persons, living or dead, events, or locales is
entirely coincidental.

ISBN 978-0-7394-7945-2

Is the
Bitch
Dead, or What?

☆ ★ ☆

1

The beige Nissan pulled slowly down 213th Street. It was a quiet, tree-lined neighborhood, where most people had manicured lawns and minded their own business. That's what Jacob Reese loved immediately about the neighborhood and that's why he decided to rent a one-family home on the block. Here he could blend into the background of the clapboard- and aluminum-sided homes, with their playing kids, their azalea bushes and maple leaf trees. Jacob was ready to start a new life.

But what happened just a few hours before could possibly upend all of his plans. He pulled into the driveway of his home. With the engine still running, he just sat in his car. Beads of sweat were still forming on his brow, threatening to run streaks down his face.

The adrenaline rush was beginning to dissipate, and Jacob

was tumbling down—crashing down. It was like coming off a crack high. He sat motionless for a moment, then grabbed the steering wheel with both hands, squeezing it so hard he started to feel pins and needles running up his forearms. He embraced the sensation.

As he gripped the steering wheel, Jacob shut his eyes as hard as he could. He wanted to stop the shaking. He wanted to squeeze out the guilt that was rushing through his body like a roaring rapid.

"That bitch! That bitch! That fucking bitch!!!!" Jacob cried out at the top of his lungs.

One neighbor next door turned off the light to his front room and peeked out the window through the blinds to see what the screaming was about. In typical New York fashion, he decided the screaming was not quite piercing enough to rate a call to 911. He closed the blinds and went to bed.

Jacob put on the black baseball cap that was in the passenger seat and prepared to go inside. He sat for a minute and reflected on what he had just done. He already regretted it. But it was over. He was mad at himself, but he was FURIOUS at Ritz Harper for being such a dumb bitch—such a smarmy, money-grubbing bitch—that people would gladly pay to see her dead.

He hated being so desperate that when the call came and the money was offered he jumped at the chance. Jacob Reese was a lot of things, but he was no killer.

He decided to do the thing he did best. He buried the thoughts he was having. Jacob was cursed with an uncanny ability to be totally delusional. He could fool himself into thinking anything he wanted. As a result, he didn't have many friends and he hadn't achieved anything in life.

Jacob wanted to be a megaproducer in the music industry. He believed he could be the next P. Diddy or Rodney Jerkins. He could see it. He knew it. Of course he could.

He was delusional.

The closest Jacob had ever come to living his dream was when he contributed eight bars to a new artist's first single. The first time he heard the finished product, Jacob convinced himself that he was the next Quincy Jones.

Jacob was always "on the scene"—hanging in the right places, going to the right parties, trying to hobnob with the right people. He partied like he owned Motown in 1968. He dressed the part. He looked the part. But the fronting was wearing thin on his psyche and his wallet. A woman can tell if a man is broke—it's in her DNA, like the mothering instinct—even if you give her all the X she can handle. Jacob had a steady supply, but not an eternal supply. One day, the keg of ecstacy would run dry, and he knew it. That was why he was desperate.

Jacob was determined to get to "the top"—whatever that meant—but he wasn't going to get there by being on the bottom of some powerful man. He was not going to be that new bitch; he was going to scratch and claw the hard way and make it on his own. Being a new bitch in the record industry wasn't much different from being a new inmate in a small cell on Rikers Island. If you come into Rikers without a rep or street credibility or much muscle or hustle, or without some-body watching your back, you are open to being eaten for lunch—literally.

In the music business, if you come in new without any rep, or anybody who will stand up for you and have your back, you are subject to being the next Bentley the Butler, with an em-phasis on the bent part, as in bent over and drilled in the butt by any mega rapper/rap mogul. There are lots of Bentley the Butlers in the music business, and very few of them actually get to be anything but. Very few of them ever get that career in the business outside of being a *Bentley*. In the record indus-try, just like in jail, you either bend over and take it, hoping for the best, or you find another way. Jacob was determined to find that way. He already had an asshole that worked just fine. He didn't need to be ripped another one.

Jacob, in his delusional mind, had other ways to suc-ceed. . . .

He got out of the car and scooted discreetly into his house. He smiled as he looked at the copy of *Confessions of a Video Vixen* on the floor of his bedroom, a book about one of those "star fuckers" whose claim to fame was that she knew how Shaq's, Jay-Z's, Vin Diesel's, and Ja Rule's dicks tasted—just like chicken!

A good read, he thought. *When I make it, I will have to look that bitch up.* He also wondered when the male version of that book was going to come out. Video hos weren't only females.

Jacob flipped open his cell phone and dialed. This partic-ular number wasn't stored in his phone and it never would be. It was a number he was to use only once, and he had to memorize it. He hesitated before dialing the number. He couldn't remember the last time he had to remember a phone number by heart. The person on the other end picked up on the second ring.

"Yo, what's good?" the voice spoke.

"It's done," said Jacob.

"Good!"

Jacob heard a click on the other end of the line. He knew that things were set. This was his first hit and he hoped it would be his last. He wasn't cut out for real shooting. He had threatened a few people but never carried it out. He had broken a few arms and legs, cracked some ribs, but he had never killed anyone. He never had a real good incentive to do so. Not even rage could bring Jacob to actually shoot somebody. But desperation and money could. He was promised two hundred and fifty thousand dollars in cash.

He had plans for his money, big plans. He was going to buy real estate and become the ultimate slumlord. He would sit back, collect fat rent checks every month, and pursue his music career.

If that didn't work out, he would focus on buying more real estate and making more money, which would give him the lifestyle he felt he deserved. He didn't want to be greedy. He didn't want to go to jail. He just wanted to have the last laugh when the semisuccessful crew he occasionally hung out with ran through all of their money and he was sitting on his, a mini Donald Trump, minus the comb-over, wallowing in dough.

Money, hos, and clothes all a nigga knows.

Jacob had a year of college under his belt, so he knew he would also have to get some sort of job to make it all legitimate. He needed to make his quarter of a million dollars clean before he tried to use it. He needed benefits. He had some dental issues that needed attending to. All those years wearing gold fronts had compromised his bottom teeth. He had at least four cavities that needed filling, and he wanted to get that Zoom whitening treatment that would make his teeth ten shades whiter, or so the advertisement said.

Jacob, in his delusional way, was very sharp when it came to knowing what women liked. He knew that women liked men who smelled good, had nice arms and circumcised dicks.

He also knew that women LOVED men who had good teeth. Once he had the money, he had to find a dentist. Tight balls were always trumped by lousy teeth!

He walked over to the pull-up bar in his bedroom doorway and took down the new suit he had hung there while he was in a rush to get to Manhattan for this job. It was a black Hugo Boss suit, shirt, and tie, still in the garment bag. It brought a smile to his face. He always wanted a nice suit. So he splurged before this job and got it in anticipation of his big payday.

"I want to look fly when I pick up my money," he said to himself. "I want to look like new money."

He hung the suit up in his tiny closet that was filled with mostly oversized polo shirts, khakis, and jeans. He promised himself more suits and more adult clothes soon.

"Hell, I'm in my thirties now. It's about time I start to look like a grown-ass man."

There was nothing childlike about his body. He didn't have a gym membership, but he regularly did calisthenics in his home. He reached up and began to do pull-ups unconsciously, losing count of how many he did, thinking only of his money—the money that would buy him his freedom, and his new teeth, and his new clothes, and the world, and all the wonders in it.

"Maddie! Maddie!"

Cecil Robinson hung up the phone and screamed for his wife, who was in the bathroom.

"What?!" Maddie responded, somewhat annoyed. "What's going on?!"

"It's Ritz, honey. Ritz has been shot! It's on TV!"

Madalyn Robinson looked haggard. She had been spending more time than she cared to in the bathroom lately. She had been on the treatments for less than two weeks, but she felt it was killing her—literally. Chemotherapy affects people in different ways, but it makes just about everyone nauseous. Chemo had hit Maddie hard. She was constantly sick. She vomited so much that her throat was raw and hoarse from the stomach acids ripping through it. She couldn't keep any food down. She lost ten pounds in less than two weeks.

"This is one diet I never wanted to be on," Maddie tried to joke with Cecil one evening. "I have been trying to lose weight my whole life, but not like this. Richard Simmons would be proud of me!"

Cecil didn't find it funny. He felt helpless watching her go through this. But he was there every step of the way for her, like he always was, like he always would be. In heaven, there is a special place for men like Cecil—quiet, dignified, hard-working, strong, responsible MEN—men who accept their responsibilities without complaint, men who take care of their own no matter what it costs, men who love their women until the day they die, men who are rocks that cannot be moved, because they are the rocks that are the foundation on which a family is built.

Men like Cecil need no great monument, or tomb, or tacky eternal flame dedicated to them when they die, because men like Cecil do not die. They live eternally in their healthy children, and their children's children, and their children's children's children, and on and on . . .

When they were "courting" back in the 1940s, Cecil and Maddie used to write each other "love letters," and Maddie of course kept them, in a little cedar box, tied in a blue ribbon, stashed in her closet. Every ten years or so, she took them out and read them.

They were so young, so innocent, so naive. Cecil wrote about how he would be satisfied to spend his life just "holding her hand"!

Maddie was very touched by that sentiment at the time,

but she and Cecil quickly learned that there was a lot more fun to be had than just "holding hands."

And that is what kept her going through the pain of the chemo. She wanted to be ready again for her baby. She wanted to look good for her man.

The real truth is never seen. The real truth, God knows, is never broadcast over the airwaves. Sexy is all about how you feel inside. It cannot be achieved through liposuction and botox. Sexy clothes don't make you sexy. Feeling good about yourself makes you sexy. And right now, Maddie didn't feel so good.

Despite that, she was still sexy to Cecil. He loved the roundness of her belly. He even loved her stretch marks. He said they made her look like a tiger, and he loved to lick them.

The thought of him doing that again—hell, just the thought of him—was what was going to keep Maddie alive, no matter what, no matter what.

The chemo had made all her hair fall out, including her thick pubic bush. Cecil had always said that her bush turned him on the most, even more than her dark erect nipples or her firm ass.

When he saw her bald pussy for the first time, he got down there, examined it, and kissed her newly exposed clit.

"You look like a tropical plant!" he said. "A Venus Flytrap! But I feel a little funny, though."

"Why?"

"Look at you. You look like a nine-year-old. I feel like a child molester!"

"Well, I can be your baby, Mr. Child Molester," Maddie said, toying with him. "Don't make me wait all night!"

And he didn't.

Maddie and Cecil loved to laugh and they loved making love. That's what they had been doing for forty years, behind closed doors, just the two of them. No one else knew what they did together, and no one would ever know.

Maddie was ready for another forty years, and maybe she would spice it up a bit when she beat the cancer and keep her pussy shaved. Or maybe she would get a Jackrabbit vibrator and do herself in front of her man. That would be something new. He would like that, she was sure.

Fuck you, Cancer!

There was a bigger malignancy in Maddie's life than the tumor that was eating away at her breast, and Maddie knew it.

Her niece, her dead only-sister's only child, had not spoken to her in more than a year. In many ways, Ritz was dead to Maddie, too. The little, sensitive, precocious child whom Maddie and Cecil loved to pieces had turned into a self-centered, vile, insensitive, malicious bitch. Maddie hoped the time away from her family would soften Ritz, help her to realize what she was missing. But it seemed to do just the opposite.

Ritz never called. Her friend Tracee did call from time to time to check up on them. Tracee had spent a weekend at Cecil and Maddie's a few years back and had such a blast that she adopted them as her own aunt and uncle. Tracee's family had moved from Jersey to California and she didn't really get along with them much. There was a story there, one Tracee never shared with anyone.

☆ ★ ☆

Tracee loved the down-home feel of the Robinsons'. She loved Aunt Maddie's mashed potatoes, whipped to perfection with just the right amount of butter and salt. She loved her sweet tea, which you only got south of the Mason-Dixon line unless you made it yourself. Tracee never understood why they never served sweet tea up north. She loved sitting on the porch after dinner in a swing chair and hearing the crickets and actually getting to see the stars in the sky, a rare sight in New York City. Being at the Robinsons' in Virginia was one of the reasons that made Tracee want to head even farther south to Florida. That felt more like her roots. While the big city, the biggest of them all—New York—had its appeal, with its opportunities, fast pace, and wall-to-wall people, the South gave you room to grow. For Tracee, who had conquered New York and made enough money to last her a lifetime, she wanted to take some time to smell the flowers, and be still, and listen to God's voice.

Tracee and Aunt Maddie often talked—just the two of them—on Saturday mornings, when Cecil would be gardening in the yard and Ritz was still in bed up in Jersey. Ritz loved to sleep, so Tracee kept Maddie and Cecil abreast of what was happening in Ritz's life while Ritz got her beauty rest.

It was Tracee who tried to get the two to reconcile, but Maddie was firm that Ritz needed to apologize and Ritz was firm that she would never apologize.

The ancient Greeks used to wonder what would happen if an irresistible force met an immovable object. Tracee wished they had discovered the answer so she could go online and look it up. She could use the solution with Ritz and Maddie.

Maddie never told Tracee that she had cancer. She knew that news might bring Ritz running back to her, but Maddie didn't want Ritz to come back like that. She wanted Ritz to change. She wanted Ritz to see herself, to see what she had become.

Years ago, Maddie and Cecil had seen a movie called *The Picture of Dorian Gray*. It was the story of a man who sold his soul in return for eternal youth, the same way Ritz had sold her soul for Arbitron ratings.

In the movie, Dorian Gray never ages, but his painted portrait does. (Back in that day, they didn't have cameras.) Every time Dorian Gray hurts someone, his portrait ages: It grows another wrinkle, it becomes more and more grotesque and ugly, until his face in the painting is nothing more than a bloated, wrinkled mask oozing pus and blood. Dorian hides the portrait in his attic and covers it with a cloth. He cannot bear to see what he really is.

Maddie wondered if Ritz had a similar covered-up portrait in her home—a picture of herself swaddled in furs and diamonds, but if you looked closely, the fur was teeming with lice, and the diamonds were just cheap glass. And her nose would look strange, too. And what about that nasty "butterfly rash" spreading across her face?

And did those once-pearly-white, thirty-five-thousand-dollar teeth now look brittle and stained and yellow?

Maddie also wondered if Ritz was aware that she had gained the world but lost her soul.

The soul . . . that was now seeping out of her life.

Maddie had to get to New York—immediately.

"Is she . . . is she . . ." Maddie couldn't get the words out as she looked at her husband.

"I don't know, Maddie," said Cecil. "Tracee called from the hospital. No one can get in to see her. We are her next of kin. We have to leave now."

Maddie gave him a puzzling look.

"I know you're not in any shape to leave now," he said. "But, Maddie, Ritzy needs us. We're all she's got."

Madalyn Robinson dug down deep and found some strength that she didn't even know she had. She went to the bathroom, took some antinausea medicine her doctor prescribed for her, took a quick shower, put on her brand-new wig and some makeup, and was waiting in the living room for Cecil within an hour.

"I'm ready, baby," she said. "I'm ready."

They could have gotten a flight out of Richmond that would put them in New York by the morning, but then they would have to catch a cab or rent a car. Cecil hated being at someone else's mercy. While everyone in New York seemed to catch cabs and ride the subway, Cecil preferred to get around in his own car. He didn't care how much it cost to park in the city. Besides, they also didn't know when they would be returning. Would they have to make funeral arrangements and go through settling Ritz's affairs and then head back to Virginia, or would they have to stay in New York for the long haul to help nurse their only niece back to health?

Madalyn also didn't know how the flight would be for her. She hadn't had a calm stomach since she started chemotherapy. In the car, they could stop at will. So Cecil threw a few things in a couple of bags for them, locked up the house, put on the alarm, left a note for Mrs. Baker next door to retrieve their papers every day, and then they hit the road.

"Maddie, no matter what we find when we get to New York, we can handle it," said Cecil. "You can do this. We've been through so much."

"Yes, baby. I know. I just pray that Ritz is alive. We should have never let all that time pass between us. Nothing should have kept us from speaking. Life is too short to be small."

Cecil let silence hang in the air. He didn't want to contemplate the brevity of life, not with his Maddie fighting for hers and now his niece, the girl he raised as his own daughter, lying in a hospital room, perhaps dead. It was almost too much for him. Cecil was never big on emotions. He was an old-school man. He provided for his family and was the pillar of the household. He was a God-fearing man of little words.

But the events of the past year—from not hearing from or

seeing Ritz to Maddie's cancer to now the shooting and possible death of Ritz—was so much more than Cecil thought he could handle. He was a strong man. He had to be as the oldest boy in a family of twelve, growing up on a farm in South Carolina. He picked cotton. He milked cows. He hauled hay. Back then, children were treated more like slaves. He never talked back to his parents, because the consequences were too great. They didn't have child welfare agencies back then, and if they did, no one was going out to the sticks and back-woods of Columbia to check on some Negro kids. And there wasn't a phone to call 911. So Cecil learned to work hard, keep his head down, and not expect too much.

He met Madalyn, this elegant, beautiful woman who gave him hope that he could have more out of this life. He left his life in South Carolina and embarked on a new adventure. He still worked hard and kept his head down, but with Madalyn he got to play. Madalyn loved to travel. Cecil had never been north of North Carolina or west of Tennessee until he met Madalyn. Together they went to Vegas, all along the strip. They went to Los Angeles and Arizona. He saw the Painted Desert and the Grand Canyon. Madalyn loved the islands, which Cecil grew to appreciate. Having worked in the hot sun most of his childhood, the idea of sitting in the hot sun didn't appeal to him much. But doing things with Madalyn made it all right. He climbed Dunn's River Falls, got on Jet Skis, and once even took a helicopter ride.

"Life is for living!" Madalyn would say. "So let's live, baby. Let's live!"

To watch her now, slowed down by sickness, broke Cecil's heart. And when her sister Gina died and little Ritz came to live with them, it gave him another source of fulfillment. He knew Madalyn could never have children and he married her anyway. He told her he grew up with enough children that the idea of fatherhood was kind of beaten out of him. But that wasn't exactly true. He loved Madalyn enough to sacrifice his desire to be a father. And while the sadness that brought Ritz to their home could not be overlooked, the joy little Ritz gave them more than made up for it. Cecil thought Madalyn was a bundle of energy. Ritz just about wore him out—but in the best way possible.

As Cecil drove up I-95, he looked over at Maddie, who was napping, with her head on a pillow against the window, and he wondered if either of his girls would ever be back to their old form. He hoped so.

3

Detective Tom Pelov grabbed Tracee gently by the arm and led her to a waiting area in an out-of-the-way part of the hospital. Pelov had investigated more than five homicides in the last six months out of this hospital and knew every nook and cranny in it. He motioned for Chas to follow.

Tracee was on the brink of hysterics and couldn't hold herself together.

"Is she . . . is she . . ." Tracee managed between shrieks of tears. "Is she dead?!"

"Please, ma'am. Please calm down," said Detective Pelov. "If we are going to find out who did this to your friend, I need you to be calm and clearheaded. I need to ask you some questions."

"Don't tell me to calm down! My friend has been shot! No one is giving us any answers! We can't get in to see her. And now you—Detective *Homicide*—want to ask *us* some questions? I think you better give us some answers first! Is Ritz dead?!"

"No. . . ."

"Good!"

"But . . . she's not out of the woods, either," said Detective Pelov. "I'm on this case because we believe that the goal of the shooter was to kill Miss Harper. We believe that person is still out there and that they will try again. I need you to help me. Now, I'm sorry, what are your names and what is your relationship to the victim?"

"The *victim's* name is Ritz Harper!" Tracee said, sniffling. She was sick and tired of all of the Jane Doe, victim stuff. "I am Tracee Remington, her best friend. I just came in town from Florida. Ritz was supposed to pick me up at the airport. Then I call got a call from Chas here at the hospital. I have no idea what's going on or who would do something like this to Ritz."

Chas was standing next to Tracee with his arms folded. He was remarkably calm and collected. He didn't want to talk to the detective. He didn't want to be at the hospital. He had business to attend to, but he couldn't look like he had someplace to go.

Detective Pelov had flipped open his notepad and was jotting down notes as Tracee spoke. He didn't look up when he asked Chas what his relationship was to the victim.

"I'm the executive producer of Ritz's radio show," Chas said.

"Do you know who may have shot Miss Harper?"

"I can't say that I do. You know her show is very provocative. She gets threats all the time. She's made a lot of folks mad."

"Who threatened her and when?"

"Wow," said Chas, looking up in the air as if he were counting those who had threatened Ritz. "That list is long. But I don't think any of them were serious."

"Obviously, at least one was serious. We need to follow all of the leads. Now, where were you when Miss Harper was shot?"

"I was in the studio, finishing up some business."

"Is that your normal routine?"

Chas hesitated. His weekday routine was to walk Ritz to her car. The two would often hang out after the show and plan the next day or the next week.

"Um, yeah. I sometimes stay behind and make some phone calls, books some guests, things like that."

"Were you alone?"

"No, our intern, Jamie, was there," Chas said.

"Okay. I need the names and contact numbers of everyone who works on the show. I also need some copies of the last week of shows. Perhaps there will be some clues in that. And if you can give me the contact information for the guests from the last couple of weeks, that would be very helpful, too."

"Do you have *any* leads?" Tracee butted in.

"There were some witnesses. We may have a partial plate and description of a vehicle. But that's it. Miss Harper's level of celebrity and notoriety actually makes this case harder.

The shooter could be literally anyone—a fan, a disgruntled guest, a friend or family member of a caller, or even someone she worked with. From what I hear, she wasn't very nice."

Tracee shot him an angry look.

"You don't know her. And I would appreciate it if you would keep your opinions to yourself!"

"It's not my opinion, ma'am," Detective Pelov said. "These are just the facts. You asked me a question. I simply answered you."

"Is there anything else we can help you with?" said Chas, looking at his watch. "I have a few things to tie up."

"Okay, that will be all," said Detective Pelov. "But please keep your cell phone on. I may need to contact you with some follow-up questions. Thank you both for your time."

Pelov put his notebook in his jacket pocket and walked away. Chas gave Tracee a hug and told her that he had to head over to the studio to prepare some sort of program to put in Ritz's time slot.

"You're leaving me here?" she said.

"I'm just a phone call away," said Chas, holding his Treo up. "If you need me, just call me. Besides, Ritz's family will be here soon."

Tracee's eyes were bloodshot from crying and lack of sleep. She was tired from the inside out and confused. She grabbed Chas's forearm.

"Do you have any idea who did this?" She looked him in his eyes.

"Baby, I wish I did. Don't worry, the cops will find whoever it is. And look around at all the security. No one is getting in here to do it again."

Tracee hadn't noticed, but there was a police officer at every entrance and exit of the hospital. No one could get in without having their bags checked and signing his or her name in a book. But was it enough? Would the shooter come back and try again?

4

The building that housed WHOT was abuzz. Reporters from every single news outlet—from television to print—flooded the lobby. They couldn't get by security in the lobby because everyone needed a pass to reach any floor. A few clever reporters managed to sneak their way to the thirty-eighth floor of the building with the hopes of finding a staircase leading to the thirty-ninth floor. It was a good plan, except that WHOT was prepared with its own security on the thirty-ninth floor, providing a dead end.

Many of the reporters even tried to bribe the security officers, hoping to just talk to anyone about the notorious Ritz Harper. They had already combed the neighborhood looking for witnesses, or anyone who could shed light on what happened the night before—the night Ritz Harper was shot on a New York City street.

"What are we going to do, Ernest?" asked Abigail Gogel, the station manager of WHOT. WHOT was started by Abigail's grandfather. The Gogel family was black but had passed for white until very recently. Abigail's grandfather was able to build an empire as a white man. Abigail was about five-three and very plump, with pale, white skin. She dyed her hair a reddish color that looked very unnatural. She could pass for a Jewish *bubula*. But every now and then, when it was convenient, Abigail would let people know she was black—like when there were minority grants or awards to get.

The station her grandfather built was bought out eight years before by a major media conglomerate that had affiliates in fifty markets. The one stipulation of the sale was that there had to be a Gogel in a well-placed position in the company. Abigail had been married twice to white men and had two sons, but she had never changed her last name.

"My family worked hard for this name and I am never going to give it up," she said to her second husband. That marriage lasted only three years. She had been single for twelve.

Abigail wasn't the most bright or savvy businesswoman. She had power because of her family legacy. The only hope of restoring any dignity to the Gogel name would be her son, Jonathan, a recent graduate of the New School who was working at the station in production. He wanted to learn the business from the bottom to the top. He wisely wanted to understand every aspect of radio. But for now, his mother was in charge. Well, sort of.

"Ernest, what are we going to do?!"

Ernest Ruffin, whom everyone called Ruff, had the title of

program director, but he was really the general manager. He handled the day-to-day issues, from the sales department to dealing with the interns to making sure the transmitter was functioning.

"Miss Gogel, don't worry. Ritz's producer has put together two weeks' worth of *Best of* shows," said Ruff. "Those will do very well, because there's so much attention right now around Ritz and the shooting that her fans are salivating to hear her voice. We have a meeting planned for later today to discuss what happens after the two weeks."

"What's her status? Is she expected to make it?"

"Um, we don't know. But it doesn't look good," said Ruff. "She took a lot of bullets in some vital places. We have a few prospects who can take her spot if that's what needs to happen."

"To be honest with you, she always made me nervous. And now with the shooting, even if she survives, perhaps we should think of replacing her," said Abigail. "She's got too much— what do the young people say?—drama around her. My grandfather built this station with a dignified vision, and I'm not about to let some loose cannon take it down. Let's seriously look for her replacement. What about Vivica Fox? Or Mo'Nique. I saw her filling in on *The View* and she was bold and had a lot to say. She has a name, and I think she could handle this job."

Ruff didn't show any expression. He was a master at wearing masks. It's why he was able to survive for the last fifteen years as program director. That was considered a lifetime in a business that was changing quickly and where program directors were beginning to take a backseat to "the talent."

Ruff was firmly in power. Everyone thought he was on their side and confided in him. He knew where all of the skeletons were buried at WHOT. That alone made him invaluable to Abigail Gogel. Ruff was also smart enough to never let her know how powerful he actually was. He pretended to defer to her on everything.

"Yes, Miss Gogel. That's a great idea," he said. "I will contact Mo'Nique's agent and see if she can fill in. If she rocks it, we should move forward with your plan. As a matter of fact, let's have Vivica Fox do one week, Mo'Nique do another week, and that hot-ass columnist Michelle Davis, the one they use as a correspondent on Fox all the time, let's try her one week. She's feisty. I think she and Ritz are friendly, too. She did a couple of pieces on Ritz, so I know she'll do Ritz a favor."

"I love it!" Abigail said. "We can promote these divas to death. . . . I mean, you know what I mean. We can get some real publicity for all of this. The best thing Ritz Harper could have done for us might have been getting herself shot."

"That's cold, Miss Gogel. That's cold."

Ruff had a smile on his face, but he didn't like Abigail. In fact, he couldn't stand her. He thought she was a dumb, fat bitch. But she never knew it. He had no intentions of replacing Ritz. Unless she died. He wanted his star back in her seat, making him look good. He knew if Ritz ever did come back, she would be bigger and better than before. He was pulling for a full recovery.

As Ruff retreated to his office, he noticed that a huge box had been delivered. He opened it to find twelve bottles of

George Vesselle champagne. It was a rosé that sold for two hundred and fifty-nine dollars a bottle.

A note inside read:

Sorry to hear about your loss. Here is something to help you soothe your pain a bit. Feel free to share it with the folks at the station. And if you need anything, a fill-in for Ritz Harper in particular, I am available.

Keep in touch,

Michelle Davis

Michelle Davis? Speak of the devil!

"What a classy lady," Ruff said to himself. "Now if she's half as good on the radio as she is on television, we may be onto something."

And what an opportunist, he thought, shaking his head. Michelle Davis already had Ritz dead, buried, and replaced— by Michelle Davis.

Ruff hadn't really thought that far in advance. He was just hoping Ritz would make it. They had enough material to do *Best of* shows. But for how long? They would need a fill-in— maybe a replacement if Ritz didn't pull through.

Michelle Davis?

Ruff tucked her card into his daily planner, put one of the bottles of George Vesselle in his office refrigerator to chill, and smiled.

She was definitely more than a possibility.

Tracee was on hour number twenty. Twenty straight hours of no sleep, no food, and very little information.

The first two hours, Tracee hadn't even seen Ritz. She wasn't allowed in because she wasn't next of kin, but she called Ritz's aunt and uncle and waited for them to drive up from Virginia. Chas was with her for a bit, but he disappeared. Then there was the detective—homicide detective—who scared the shit out of her, having her think Ritz was dead. He was, however, one of the few bright spots in her evening, because he came back to the hospital and stayed with her and comforted her. At least he was trying to get to the bottom of this mystery.

No one knew anything, and if they did, they weren't telling Tracee anything about Ritz's progress or condition. It was frustrating.

When Madalyn and Cecil arrived, Tracee immediately noticed how haggard Aunt Madalyn looked. She gave them both a huge hug and they sat down in the waiting area, hoping a doctor would come by.

"How was your trip?" asked Tracee, straining to make small talk to keep her mind and theirs, too, off the serious issues before them.

"Oh, it wasn't too bad," said Cecil. "There wasn't much traffic. We made it in just six hours, which is pretty good."

Aside from Madalyn's appearance, another strange thing that Tracee noticed was the silence. Ritz's Aunt Madalyn was known for having the gift of gab. She could talk twenty-four/seven about any- and everything, but she hadn't said more than two words since she arrived. At first Tracee thought that Aunt Madalyn was taking the shooting really hard. But there seemed to be something else.

"Are you okay, Aunt Madalyn? What's the matter?"

"Oh, nothing, baby. Nothing for you to worry about," Madalyn said, seeing the lines of concern etching their way across Tracee's brow.

"I'm going to go find a doctor, but I think you guys need to go someplace and rest. Ritz is going to need your strength," Tracee said. "You're more than welcome to stay at my loft. I have plenty of room and I would love to have you. It may be a bit dusty, though. I haven't been there in a while."

"Oh, we're just going to check into a hotel around the corner," Uncle Cecil said. "No need to put you out."

"You two could *never* put me out. I would be honored if you stayed with me. Really. I'd love the company."

"You're so sweet, Tracee, but I want to be close to Ritz in case she needs us. I want to be minutes away," Madalyn said.

The truth was that Madalyn didn't want Tracee to see her morning treatments and the sickness that followed. There was enough going on, and Madalyn wanted to make sure that everyone focused their attention and energy on Ritz, and Ritz only.

Tracee found a doctor and the three of them tried to see Ritz through a glass, but they really couldn't see anything behind all the machines and curtains. Dr. Paul Grevious didn't want anyone in the room. Not until she was out of the woods. It was too risky. Since they weren't able to spend any time with Ritz, Aunt Madalyn and Uncle Cecil decided to make their way around the corner and check into a hotel. Against their wishes, Tracee accompanied them to the hotel and insisted on putting the room on her credit card. She made sure they were comfortable and told them that she'd check on them later.

"Please get some rest, you two," Tracee said. "I love you."

"We love you, too," Aunt Madalyn said. The three exchanged hugs and Tracee headed back to the hospital.

Tracee was determined to get in and really see Ritz. She needed to see for herself what was up. Tracee staked out Ritz's room and waited for the nurses' shifts to change. When a nurse finally left her post, Tracee saw her chance and took it. She slipped into Ritz's room.

What Tracee saw made her instantly burst into tears. Ritz was totally unrecognizable.

Her entire face was swollen. She looked like Mitch "Blood" Green after Mike Tyson busted his ass one night outside of Dapper Dan's clothing store in Harlem. She had tubes going in and out of what seemed like every orifice of her body. One of her eyes was swollen to three times its normal size and there was purple all around it. She was on a breathing pump and all kinds of gadgets monitored her heart and blood pressure. Ritz didn't just look bad, she looked dead, and that was what had Tracee spooked.

She let out a wail, and a moment later, a nurse came scurrying into the room.

"What are you doing in here?!" the nurse said in an angry voice.

"That's my best friend. Is she going to make it?" Tracee said through uncontrollable sobs. "She looks so bad. She looks so bad."

"Miss, I'm going to have to ask you to leave. Please come this way."

The nurse grabbed Tracee by the arm. Tracee pulled away and got closer to Ritz's bedside. She just wanted to touch her to see if she was alive. Tracee grabbed Ritz's hand.

"Please, God, spare her life," Tracee cried out. "Please, God, pleeeeeeeease!"

As the nurse was trying to pull Tracee away, Ritz's heart monitor began to quicken its pace.

Beep.Beep.Beep.Beeeeeeeeeeeeeeeeeeeeep!

The nurse became a little more physical, pushing Tracee from the room, and then doctors and orderlies and nurses came rushing in with all kinds of equipment and trays and needles.

"Oh God, no! No! No!" Tracee screamed.

6

What the fuck?

That was all Ritz Harper could muster in her mind, which was racing at a million miles per hour. Amid the cacophony of thoughts, only one thought kept resounding, only one thought rang out like a gong inside her head: *What the fuck?!*

Ritz could not feel a thing. There was no pain. But if she strained, she could hear a faint beep that seemed to be far off in the distance.

Ritz Harper, who had worked her way to the top of her game, who was the undisputed queen of all media, the most talked-about woman in America, now was flat on her back and silenced.

"Okay. Okay. Okay!" Ritz screamed. Only, no sound came out of her mouth. The beep was becoming more rapid.

Where am I? She was trying to gain some kind of control.

Make some sense of this confusion. Her thoughts were lucid, but she battled consciousness. Was she conscious? Was she even alive?

Beep. Beep. Beeeeeeeeeeeeeeeeeeeeeeeep!

A bright light appeared out of the corner of nowhere. The light was surrounded by rings. The rings looked watery, like the rings made when a pebble is tossed into the center of a pond. There were translucent ripples around the light.

A figure appeared through the ripples. It was a feminine figure. The figure was saying something, but to Ritz it sounded like a record slowed down on a turntable. It was like a seventy-eight recording played at forty-five speed—slow and warped. Then, just as suddenly, everything was in sync.

"Ritzy?" The voice had sped up to flow with real time. "Ritzy? Sweetie."

"Ma?!" Ritz could feel a lump build in her throat that almost choked her. In that moment, Ritz was ten years old again. "Mama?"

"Yes, baby girl. It's me."

"Oh, Mama! I—I—I've missed you so much."

"I know, baby. I know."

"I've needed you so much!"

Was she dreaming? Ritz wasn't sure and didn't care. She had always heard of people contacting the dead and vice versa. Hell, *Ghost* was one of her favorite movies, even if she felt that Whoopi should have won her Oscar for *The Color Purple*.

But Ritz lived in the real world where things like that never happened. She even had a friend in college who said she could see spirits. But Ritz didn't believe any of that. Because if people could see spirits, then why had she never seen her mother? Why didn't her mother try to contact her? So spirits couldn't be real.

But here she was looking at her mother in a surreal environment with funny light. She could almost see through her mother, but she was there, standing in front of Ritz. She was so close that Ritz reached out to touch her.

"Ritzy, believe it or not, I've always been there," her mother said. "I've always been watching over you."

"How?" Ritz said. "Where? Why didn't I know it? And if you've always been there, why didn't you warn me, tell me to run or duck before I got shot? Why didn't you stop this from happening to me? Why didn't you stop so many things from happening to me?"

Ritz was mad at her mother. More than twenty years' worth of anger and other emotions came flooding back.

"Baby, it's not that simple. I could only watch. I've seen it all. Everything."

Ritz felt a little heat of shame rise up in her. She could literally see her life passing before her eyes, and she didn't like what she was seeing: the night she slept with Jamie's boyfriend, Derek; the night she destroyed Delilah Summers; the day she outed a successful rapper, ruining his career; the day she outed a minister, throwing his family and congregation into a tizzy; the time she made an up-and-coming actress admit on the air that she had herpes, reducing her to tears and all but destroying her future in films.

But to Ritz, those were minor incidents. What really stood out was a flashback to the argument she had with her Aunt Maddie, the woman who raised her after Ritz's mother died. It was a nasty argument. It should never have happened. It had spun out of control.

Ritz had been wrong. She knew that now. If she was honest, deep down, she always knew that.

"Wrong and strong!" her mother used to tease Ritz when she would get in trouble, because Ritz never backed down when she was wrong, even when she knew damn well that she was wrong. Ritz felt bad for the things she said to Aunt Maddie, who only showed her love and always wanted the best for her.

Her aunt had only questioned why Ritz wanted to destroy her former friend, Delilah Summers. Aunt Maddie simply couldn't understand Ritz's ambition, her desire to be on top at any cost. Aunt Maddie and Uncle Cecil hadn't raised her that way. Maddie couldn't understand Ritz's level of envy and injustice that someone like Delilah could have so much success—success that Ritz believed should have been for her. Why couldn't Aunt Maddie understand? Ritz's envy stemmed from a sense of injustice; Delilah's success should have been Ritz's, and she didn't understand why Aunt Maddie just didn't get it.

Why did she push me like that? Ritz thought. *She should have understood.*

Wrong and strong. Strong but wrong. In other words, wasted strength—strength that could have been used in such better ways.

All Aunt Maddie knew was that Ritz wasn't raised to be like that. Ritz was raised to be a lady, not a diva. Aunt Maddie wasn't even quite sure what a diva was—to her, a diva was a fat woman who sang at the opera—but she didn't like it, and she knew that Ritz's mother would not have liked it, either.

Almost as if she could read Ritz's mind, her mother said, "Don't worry, baby. No judgment. Everything we do in life, good or bad, leads to a lesson or a blessing. Some of us have to learn our lessons the hard way. That has always been your way. And everything we do, baby, everything we do has a consequence."

Ritz took a minute to let that thought sink in.

"That sounds like it's my fault that I got shot. So am I here now because of something I did? And where am I exactly? Am I dead? Is this heaven? Where's God . . ."

"Slow down. I'll answer most of your questions, but some of the questions you will have to answer for yourself," said Ritz's mother as she put her arm around Ritz's shoulder, a tender gesture that Ritz didn't actually expect to feel.

But Ritz could feel her mother's touch, hear her mother's voice. And the air where they were had a scent. It was sweet, with a light hint of lavender.

"First, you are not dead, not really. You aren't alive, either. You are able to see me because you have left your physical body in that hospital room. I wanted to make sure I was here to send you back."

"So I'll live?"

"Yes, you'll live. But before I send you back, I need to tell you some things. Baby, you have to think about what you're doing with your life. You'll be given a second chance. But *please* make the most of it. You were put on earth to do some incredible things, Ritzy. You're a leader. People will follow you. But with that comes a lot of responsibility. Remember when I used to tell you that your mouth would get you in trouble?"

"Yes, I remember . . . but you know I didn't mean anything bad when I talked back."

"That's not the point, baby. Whether you intend for bad things to happen, your mouth makes them happen. Words are powerful. When you say something, it goes somewhere. And it usually comes right back. You have to learn how to control your words. Use them wisely. You can't say everything you want to say. You've hurt people. You've destroyed families and lives with your words. You don't see that? You don't see the tears and the broken hearts and the broken souls that you've caused? I see it and I cry. I cry for them, and I cry for you."

"What about *my* tears? What about *my* hurt? What about *my* broken heart?" said Ritz.

"Baby, making others feel that way won't make *your* pain go away. It never does. It only brings more pain to you in the end. I didn't say you got what you deserved. Nobody deserves to be shot. Nobody deserves to be killed. Nobody deserves to be hurt, physically or emotionally—no one.

"I said that you hurt people, and now *you've* been hurt.

There's a relationship between what you've done and what's been done to you, and you have to examine that. You need to start asking yourself questions. You need to find out if it's more important to be what you think is a 'success' in this world, or is it more important to be a person worthy of the people who follow you? Which person is my Ritzy? When you figure that out, you will know what to do."

"I'm so confused, Mama. I am so angry. I'm angry at a world that tells you that you have to be a certain way to get to the top. I'm angry that when I was just good at my job, it wasn't good enough. When I was better than everyone and worked harder, it didn't get me ahead. I'm angry that it's a man's world and that I have to act like a man sometimes to get where I want to go. I'm angry that I can't find a man who completely understands me and accepts me. I'm angry that even my best friend doesn't get it. And I'm angry at you, Mama. I'm mad as hell that you left me all alone to try to figure this shit out for myself. Why did you do that? Why did you leave me?! Why?!!!"

Ritz broke into an uncontrollable cry. She cried as if her soul were dying. She had not cried like this since her mother died. She would whimper from time to time on occasion, when she would throw herself a small, but private, pity party. But those parties were infrequent. Ritz didn't allow herself to do much self-reflection or assessment. But she did believe in KIM—Keeping It Moving. KIM was Ritz's favorite hang-out partner. KIM never looked back, never made any excuses, and never asked for apologies.

Ritz's sobs seemed to want to drown her, which was strange, being in limbo between life and death. She couldn't feel any physical pain, but her emotions were so raw, she felt like her insides had been shredded and alcohol and salt had been poured on her wounds.

"Why, Mama?!"

Ritz's mother held her like the little baby she once was, rocking her back and forth.

"Baby, you're asking me something people have been asking since the dawn of man. You're asking me why I died. I can't answer that. I don't really know why. What I do know is what I told you before—everything happens for a reason. You're either getting a lesson or a blessing. Ritz, my death didn't happen to you. I didn't leave you. I died. It wasn't my choosing, believe me. And I didn't leave you, because I've always been here. Right here."

She spread her hand over Ritz's heart.

"I've always been inside of you. Everything I have ever said to you since you were a baby is all inside you. My DNA is in you. I never left you. But that was a lesson I guess you never learned. Maddie tried to tell you that when she said I didn't raise you to be that way. She was trying to get you to remember who you were. She was trying to get you to remember that I was inside of you, always."

Ritz's spirit was heaving as she tried to regain control and process what her mother was saying. She still didn't want to hear it. Ritz wanted her mother to tell her why she abandoned her, and she wasn't getting the answers she was looking for.

"And believe this, baby girl. By the time I left the earth, you had the foundation to handle everything the world would throw at you. The things I instilled in you before I left were more than enough for you to build on. And I gave you my sister—one of the most incredible people ever born—to balance you out. Everything that I wasn't, Maddie is. There were things to learn from her that you ignored. But you have time. Not much time, but you will have time. You will have all the time you need."

"Mama, I don't care about time with them! I want time with *you*! We didn't have enough time, Mama. We didn't have enough time!"

Ritz's mother smiled. "Wrong and strong," she said gently. "We had enough time. Compared to so many, we had so much time. Maybe not as much time as you would have liked, but more than enough time. We knew each other. We loved each other. I rocked you to sleep in my arms. I heard you tell me that you loved me. We were so blessed."

"Mama, don't go. . . ."

"My baby, I have never gone. I will never go. When will you understand that?"

"Mama!"

"Don't be sad, beautiful girl. Be happy. Now you know the secret."

"What secret?"

"The secret that will set you free: To know ultimate happiness, you must first know ultimate despair. You must first know what it feels like to die before you can truly appreciate how glorious it is to live.

"From now on, no more 'wrong and strong,' baby girl. From now on, it's 'right and strong.' I love you so much, Ritgina. I love you so much. . . ."

Ritgina. Mama had called her Ritgina. Why? She usually only called her by her birth name when Ritz had done something wrong.

Ritz felt her body jerk like she was being sucked into a vacuum cleaner. Her mother's voice became warped again, like a slowed-down recording. And translucent ripples blurred the image. Ritz could no longer feel her mother's touch. She couldn't smell the lavender. She could hear the heart monitor and through her lids see bright lights. And suddenly she felt pain. She felt physical pain and it was excruciating. She felt an electric bolt rip through her chest. She felt like she was on fire. She heard a man's voice say, "Clear!" And the bolt of lightning ripped through her once again.

Beep. Beep. Beep.

Ritz heard the steady beep of the heart monitor, and the chaos around her was settling into a calm.

"She's back," the man's voice said. "She's alive."

The collect call came in at around nine in the evening, as it always did. Call from inmate number 96636.

"Yes, I'll accept," Derek said.

"Hey, li'l bro!" It was Jayrod, Derek's brother, who was facing fifteen years for tax evasion related to his drug dealing. "Yo, thank you for taking care of that little thing for me!"

Jayrod couldn't say much more, because every letter, every correspondence, every single phone call was monitored from prison. The last thing he was going to do was implicate himself in a murder. He did, however, find some joy at the misfortune that befell Ritz Harper, and he wanted to let his brother know how much he appreciated him.

"Yeah, um. So how are you doing?" Derek wanted to change the subject.

"I'm feeling so good," Jayrod said. "The next thing on my

list is getting a new trial so I can get the fuck out of here. I mean, I'm well taken care of, but brother, this ain't home. And I'm itching to get back home. Can you imagine us riding side by side? We'll take over the world!"

Derek was uncomfortable with the notion of him and Jayrod "reunited," like Peaches & Herb. There was a part of him that really didn't want Jayrod to come home. Derek was running the business fine—better than fine, actually. He was able to take the enterprise to another level, a level that Jayrod could never attain.

He and his brother had totally different styles: Jayrod was loud, temperamental, and flashy. Derek was smooth and quiet. Jayrod would want to pick up where they left off. Derek had moved on, way, way on. He was looking forward to taking his profits and buying a few Laundromats and going completely legit.

Jayrod would never, ever be legit, and Derek knew that.

"How's that's honey dip of yours? She keeping you satisfied?"

"We're doing okay. I'm thinking about cooling things, though."

"Yeah. Fuck her. She served her purpose, right?"

That statement could be taken a couple of ways. Derek wasn't going to respond.

"I'll be up to see you next week, and I'm going to make a little deposit into your account tomorrow."

"That's my baby brother! I love you, man. Thank you so much again. I just wanted you to know that having you out there for me makes it a little bit easier to do this time in here."

"I love you, too," Derek said. "I'll see you next week."

"Peace out!"

The phone went dead, and Derek was glad. Jayrod thought that Derek had dealt with the "Ritz Bitch." She was shot. She should be dead. Jayrod assumed that his wishes had been granted. He just assumed that wishing would make it so.

That was the problem with Jayrod. He assumed too much—and that is why when he finally did get out, it would be just a matter of time before he'd go back.

Derek smiled, remembering a little saying that he learned from Miss Montpelier, his third-grade teacher: When you ASSUME, you make an ASS out of U and ME.

Derek hated to think it, but Jayrod was an ass. He loved his brother, but his brother was a jailbird, a convicted felon, and quite frankly, not the sharpest pencil in the box.

Derek was a Mont Blanc and was not going to have his nice life ruined by a Bic, someone who "assumed" that he could have someone killed.

Especially if that someone was Ritz Harper.

Derek couldn't tell Jayrod that he had nothing to do with the shooting of Ritz Harper. He never hired anyone to do it. He couldn't—not after the night they spent together. He couldn't tell his brother that he was actually really messed up by her shooting, that he wanted to rush to the hospital and see her, that he was hoping she would live. He couldn't tell him any of that. His brother hated Ritz so much. He wanted to hate her, too, but he got to see a side of her that his dick could never forget.

☆　★　☆

Who would have known that a drop he had to make in a fancy Jersey neighborhood would be literally in Ritz's backyard?

He was stuck at the front gate of Ritz's gated community as the guard was calling his customer. Going through the residents' gateway was a beautiful Aston Martin Vanquish. The person in the car slowed down and stopped right next to Derek. The window went down, and there was Ritz Harper.

"Derek? What are you doing here? How did you know where I lived?"

"I didn't. I'm doing some business out here," he said.

"Where's your little girlfriend?" she said.

Derek rolled his eyes and didn't respond. Ritz was being playful, but he didn't want to give in to her whims. Ritz got out of her car, walked over to Derek's window, and leaned in. She let her double Ds flop out of her blouse—not too much, but just enough to get Derek to stare at them.

"It seems as though your little business friend isn't responding. You want to come over and wait until they get in?"

Derek was a little surprised. But in his line of work he had learned to never be surprised, ever. He nodded. Ritz told the guard that Derek was with her, then he followed her through the gate and up the hill to her home. Ritz's house was everything Derek imagined—glamorous and over the top.

They sat down on a plush sofa. She asked him what he wanted to drink.

"Just a glass of ice water, with lots of ice," he said.

Ritz came back with a tall, slim glass of ice water and a cocktail glass filled with Grey Goose. Ritz loved to unwind when she was home alone. She would have a drink on occasion and would definitely smoke a little weed, which was her little secret.

She took a seat on her plush, suede couch right next to Derek. She was practically sitting on top of him. He shifted in his seat to give her more room. She inched closer.

"Do you have any weed?" Ritz boldly asked. "I know you must."

"Why do you know I must?" Derek asked sheepishly. "All black men don't sell weed or even know where to get weed!"

Ritz shot him a look that said, *Do you think I'm stupid?*

"Come on, let me see what you got," Ritz said, reaching across his pants to dig in his pocket, ignoring his fake indignation.

He grabbed her hand and held it.

"It's not in my pocket. I don't keep shit on me," Derek said, letting her hand go.

He got up and went outside to his Jeep. He had a hidden compartment underneath the seat. He took out a small bag and came back into the house. He unrolled the bag and took out a piece of hemp rolling paper. It was very thin and didn't intrude on the weed. It was like smoking without the paper. Derek laid the paper out flat and crumbled some of his best skunk out on the paper. The weed was perfect. It was already presorted for sticks and lumps. He rolled a flawless joint with his thumbs in one motion. He lightly licked the edge to make it stick and smoothed it out with his fingers.

It was the best-looking joint Ritz had ever seen. When she rolled her own, they looked lumpy and uneven. She didn't care before. It all smoked the same, she thought. But when she lit up Derek's, she realized that they didn't all smoke the same. She inhaled deeply, and in a matter of minutes she was in another place. Derek looked at her and smiled.

"Nice, huh?" he said.

"This is the best shit I've ever had. No wonder you're so successful," said Ritz.

"How do you know I'm successful?" he said.

She gave him another *What, do you think I'm stupid?* look. And he smiled again. Derek wasn't much of a smiler, but he was smiling a lot this night. He grabbed his glass and took a swig of his water. Ritz was completely ignoring her drink and was being very selfish with the joint. Derek didn't mind. He wasn't much of a smoker. He liked to have his wits about him at all times.

She laid the joint in the stylish Orrefors ashtray on her coffee table and leaned over and kissed him. It was an urgent kiss. Derek pierced her mouth with his tongue, which was cold from the ice water, then heated up her entire mouth. The sensation was weird and arousing. Ritz gripped the back of his head and raked her nails firmly down his neck and then down his back. She could feel the hard ripples of his muscles through his shirt—which was irritatingly in the way. Ritz pulled back and told him to take it off.

Derek got up, and Ritz leaned back and watched him like she was watching a striptease. Derek purposely took his time unbuttoning his Ralph Lauren button-down, taking a second at each button. Ritz was eager, but she was too mature to show it. She was going to let him play. She was having fun. She lit and took another drag of the joint, and as he pulled his undershirt over his head she let out a steady stream of smoke.

"Boy, you sure are blessed," Ritz said, her breath quickening.

"No, baby, this is hard work," he said. Derek looked like one of those posters they have in the gym of what a perfect body is supposed to look like. Every muscle was uniquely defined, covered in the most beautiful, smooth skin. He was one of those brothers who has a hard time growing a full beard and doesn't have much body hair, just one straight strip leading into his jeans, like a runway. Ritz grabbed him by his belt and pulled him close to her.

"I got the rest," she said.

Now it was her turn to tease. She undid his belt and pulled it all the way out of the belt loops. She opened the button on his jeans and inched his zipper down. His bulge was so big, it was like Ritz had unleashed a python after she had gotten the zipper all the way down. His pants fell to his ankles. She slid her hands around his perfect ass and pulled down his cotton boxers. She took her tongue and, starting at the base of his shaft, licked all the way, all ten inches. Derek let out a moan. His knees almost buckled. Ritz then pulled him onto the couch, facedown.

"What the fuck?" Derek said. He didn't like that position at all. But lying facedown, his ass exposed, gave him a thrill that he was not able to acknowledge—yet.

"Trust me," Ritz said, as she climbed on top of him from behind and whispered in his ear. She had gotten her clothes off in a split second and was rubbing her huge breasts down the small of his back. Her nipples were swollen and erect, and she loved how they felt on his skin.

Derek's dick was pulsing like it had its own respiratory system. He wanted to be inside her—he had to have that wet, warm, silky tightness around his dick. She was on top of his back, kissing him. He was reacting to nature, and involuntarily humping the couch. He couldn't stop—she kissed, he thrust. He wanted to throw her on her back and then fuck her like a man. He didn't want to cream on the couch cushions! And if he did, would she send him the dry cleaner's bill?

Ritz ran her tongue down the small of his back to the crack of his ass. She parted his cheeks with her tongue and plunged it into his ass. Derek had never felt anything like it. He couldn't take it anymore. He flipped over, grabbed his jeans, reached into his pocket, and pulled out a Magnum. Ritz grabbed for it. But Derek already had it on.

"Not so quick," she said.

"Don't worry, I'm definitely going to take my time. You're going to have to come for this." The double meaning wasn't lost on Ritz, who simply closed her eyes at the thought.

Derek took a moment to stare at Ritz and really look at

her. *Behind all of that fake shit, she is really beautiful,* he thought to himself. Her skin was flawless. Her pubic area was perfectly manicured. The Brazilian wax job had taken care of that very well.

Derek reached into his glass of water and fished out an ice cube. He ran the ice over Ritz's chest and then over her nipples. He was right behind every stroke of ice with his warm tongue and mouth. He would put out a fire with the ice and start a new one with his mouth. Ritz couldn't keep still. She was writhing and wiggling with each stroke. She opened her mouth to say something, and Derek rubbed the ice cube over her lips and licked off the dripping water and plunged his tongue into her mouth. Ritz gasped with pleasure. Ritz grabbed him and tried to direct him on top of her, but he promised he was going to take his time and he meant it. He grabbed another cube of ice and rubbed it lightly over her engorged clit. He pushed the cube into her blazingly hot opening. And Ritz thought she was going to explode. He followed with his tongue, which he dipped into the iced hot spot and then slowly swirled it around her about-to-burst clit. Ritz grabbed his head. She was holding on for mercy. Derek flicked her clit ferociously with his tongue until Ritz knew she was going to explode. She needed to feel him inside of her. She had to have him right then.

With all of her strength, Ritz pulled Derek on top of her. He followed willingly this time. She guided his hips over her to the perfect spot. She grabbed his ass and plunged him inside of her with all of her might. He was so big and she was so ready. Ritz wrapped her legs around him and he expertly went to work, hitting every single chord in her symphony. Ritz thought she might have lost consciousness for a second. She came almost immediately the first time, and then two more times before Derek was done.

Derek had been with quite a few women—most of whom knew how to put their thing down. But Ritz Harper? *She is a bad bitch*, Derek thought, as she lay on the suede couch exhausted. *Now what?*

The two didn't exchange words. Derek gave her a juicy kiss on her lips. He got dressed. He checked his cell. There was a message from his customer apologizing for being late.

"I got to run, babe," Derek said, cool but still very woozy from the experience.

"Okay. Maybe we'll catch up again sometimes," Ritz said, trying to be equally cool, but also very woozy from the experience.

Derek left the bag of weed on the coffee table and left. He saw Ritz a couple of nights after that when Jamie asked him to come up to the studio to pick her up. Ritz did her usual flirting, but she acted as if that night never happened. Derek slipped and blushed when Ritz said hello. But it was so quick, he didn't think anyone noticed. Ritz did. And so did Jamie.

Ritz was now shot, maybe dead. And what about Jamie? He would have to break up with her. He liked her too much to string her along. She deserved better. Derek was too distracted to be in a relationship—too distracted by his business, too distracted by Ritz.

He had to make the break from Jamie quick and clean. He needed to be away from the whole scene, fade back into his world and disappear.

Edwin had nervous energy most Sunday mornings, but it was mostly excitement. He would prepare his sermons during the week. But Sunday morning, standing in the pulpit, he may be overcome with the spirit and everything he had written would be out the window. It was the unpredictability, the unexpected that may happen on any given Sunday. He might look out and see a face in the crowd and be inspired to preach about something totally different than planned. He may hear someone at the altar call out for prayer for a particular thing that might inspire Edwin to preach about that. With all of his scholarly learning and preparation from Drew University, what went on in the pulpit on a Sunday could not be taught or anticipated. Pastors are made and broken based on their ability to make that magical moment happen on Sunday.

This Sunday would be perhaps the most unpredictable of

his career. It was Edwin's first sermon since his life was up-ended. In just one afternoon, everything he worked for, everything he was born to do was thrown into jeopardy. His entire life—his family, his ministry, his world—was changed forever. Thanks to Ritz Harper. It was on her show that a man he once knew long before he was Pastor Edwin Lakes, head of one of the biggest churches in New York City, and grow-ing into one of the biggest in the country, revealed that he was in love with Edwin. This man said that he had a relation-ship with Edwin and that Edwin left him abruptly without so much as a good-bye. The man had been harboring these feel-ings for years and just had to let it out.

Actually, the man's story was masterfully pulled out of him by Ritz Harper, whose entire career was built on ruining lives with rumor, innuendo, and gossip. But this story happened to be the truth—truth that would be better served untold. But it was a truth that also needed an explanation.

Edwin debated addressing it at all. But he had to. His min-istry was built on the Word. And the Word was rooted in truth. His church family deserved that much. They deserved it as much as his wife deserved to hear it from his mouth instead of from some stranger on the radio. Edwin had very few regrets in life, but he regretted not telling his wife about his experiences in Miami, Florida, where for a few glorious months he had more fun than he could ever imagine and had had a relationship with another man.

How could he have explained it to her? What would he have said? How would he even have brought it up? He decided that the Miami affair had no impact on his life. It was over. He never looked back and didn't reminisce about that time. Not one moment. He loved his life and he loved his wife. Why burden her with doubt?

No one ever believes that you can have a homosexual experience and completely walk away. Pastor Donnie Mc-Clurkin admitted that he used to be a homosexual and he couldn't stop being the butt of some comedian's jokes. It just seems impossible. But it's not. Edwin completely walked away from that life. But he didn't trust Patricia to believe him. Not telling her the truth was not only a mistake, it was un-Jesus-like. Whether Patricia believed him or not, he had an obligation to tell her the truth. He had to know that their love could conquer all. Now, as he prepared to go it alone for the first Sunday since he got married, he wasn't so sure if their love could conquer this.

Edwin missed his family dearly. They made his Sunday mornings less hectic. He would start with a lovemaking session with his beautiful wife. Morning sex was the best, he always thought. It was a perfect way to start a day. Even though that was their routine, it was never routine, it was never mundane, it was never rote. It was always loving. It always hit the spot—both their spots.

Then, afterward, the banter of his children around the breakfast table—not to mention the nice breakfast of scrambled eggs and turkey bacon with whole-grain toast—is what gave Edwin's life meaning. Edwin loved his life. He loved the order of it.

Not having his family this particular Sunday left such a hole in his spirit, but somehow it seemed appropriate.

"When Jesus was about to be crucified, he brought his disciples with him and they all fell asleep," Edwin said to himself. "I guess the lesson is when you have something tough to face, sometimes you'll have to face it alone. I have to handle this situation by myself."

Edwin's mother and a few other members of the church tried to come around to comfort him. But he ignored them. They were just distractions and crutches, and he needed neither.

He would have to face his entire congregation and explain to them why their pastor had a homosexual relationship and he'd have to tell them why he was still worthy of being their pastor.

He sat at his huge wooden desk in his inner sanctuary, lined with rich oak paneling and oak bookcases, filled with Bibles from all over the world and the spiritual writings of many different faiths. The floors were wall-to-wall with plush crimson carpeting. Edwin studied his sermon. It was filled with passages about forgiveness and judgment. Would this get through to them?

He did what he always did right before going out to the pulpit. He kneeled at a small altar in the corner of his office and he prayed. He prayed.

"Heavenly Father, thank You for giving me another day on this earth to do Your will. Grant me the eloquence You gave your servant Moses. Grant me the wisdom You gave

Your servant Solomon, and grant me the strength of the Lord Almighty. Encamp Your angels around this church and open the minds and hearts of everyone who hears my voice, Lord. Let the truth be ever present. In Jesus Christ's name I pray. Amen."

Edwin took a deep breath and headed into the sanctuary, not knowing what to expect. The organist was playing something that Edwin couldn't really hear. The choir was singing something, too. But Edwin was caught up in his thoughts. He took his seat next to the pulpit. It was a big wooden throne-like seat, where his father had once sat. Edwin remembered being in the front pew, looking up at his father and thinking he looked like a god. He was larger than life. Edwin used to wonder what he would look like up there one day. But this day he didn't care what he looked like.

When the music stopped, Edwin got up and stood behind the pulpit. He stood there for what seemed like an eternity, not saying a word. It was as if he wanted to look into the eyes of each and every one of his congregants. The church was packed, more packed than usual. It was full of not just members, but also curiosity seekers and about a dozen news reporters standing in the back. There wasn't a seat available. It was standing room only. Edwin had never seen so many people in one service. But there was one person whom Edwin wanted desperately to see—his wife.

Since they had been married, not less than four hours passed without them speaking. Now it had been two days since Edwin had heard from his family. Patricia's mother had given Edwin an update, telling him Patricia needed more time. He understood. Everything she believed in had been ripped from her. Edwin wasn't just her husband, he was her pastor, her connection to God. That, too, was hanging in the balance, but Edwin was going to make it all right again, he hoped.

Edwin steadied himself and placed his hand on the side of the pulpit. With his other hand, he unbuttoned his collar, then unzipped his robe and let it fall to the floor. He stood there with his crisp, white dress shirt and royal-blue tie with silver specks. It was a tie Patricia had picked out for him at Brooks Brothers, and it was his favorite. He loosened the tie, cleared his throat, and began to speak.

"I took off this robe because I am here before you naked. I am not your pastor this morning. I am one of the flock. I am just a man. I have always been just a man. I know many of you are here today more out of curiosity and the desire to know something that—quite frankly—is none of your business. Some of you are here out of glee, hoping to see a fallen man, and you want to see whether or not that fallen man can get up again and walk again. I see that our church is filled to capacity, with many new people here.

"Maybe we should have sold tickets and charged our new friends a hundred dollars for admission. No, make that five hundred. On second thought, make that *a thousand* dollars a pop. They would have paid that, gladly. And think of what all that money could do for our annual Help the Homeless campaign!"

The congregation—as one—gasped.

Most of them were expecting Edwin to do a Jimmy Swaggart, forgive-me-lord-for-I-have-sinned routine, complete with bended knees and crocodile tears, like when the televangelist got caught in a motel room with a two-dollar-an-hour hooker, whom he paid to watch him masturbate.

"Well, I hate to disappoint you. But this sermon today is only for people who love God and who serve him. Turn with me if you will to the Book of John, Chapter Eight. We will start with Verse Three. The New International Version reads:

> *The teachers of the law and the Pharisees brought in a woman caught in adultery. They made her stand before the group and said to Jesus, "Teacher, this woman was caught in the act of adultery. In the Law Moses commanded us to stone such women. Now what do you say?" They were using this question as a trap, in order to have a basis for accusing him.*
>
> *But Jesus bent down and started to write on the ground with his finger. When they kept on questioning him, he straightened up and said to them, "If anyone of you is without sin, let him be the first to throw a stone at her."*

"Now, most people stop there. And I am going to talk about the throwing of the stones, but the meat of this scripture comes a little later. After Jesus tells those without sin to cast the first stone, He continues to write with his finger on the ground. I guess he was writing out the sins of those before him, just in case someone decided to lie and stone her anyway. Each one of those men walked away one by one. I also found it interesting that if the woman was caught in adultery, where was the man she was caught in adultery with? And why wasn't he brought forth to be stoned? But Jesus deals with this directly when He is left there alone with the woman to be stoned. In Verse Ten, Jesus stands up and asks her:

> *"Woman, where are they? Has no one condemned you?"*
> *"No sir," she said.*
> *"Then neither do I condemn you," Jesus declared. "Go now and leave your life of sins."*

"Many of you are here today to throw stones at me. And it would be easy for me to stand before you and tell you that whoever is without sin can do so. I'm sure there will be a few toddlers sent up here carrying rocks too big for them to handle."

A wave of chuckles carried throughout the church. It was the first time the church members were able to release any energy. Usually when Edwin started his sermon, the Amen Corner started early. You have those folks in every church who want to be heard agreeing with everything the pastor says, amen-ing and mmm-hmm-ing throughout the whole sermon. On this morning you could hear a pin drop until Edwin broke the ice with his little joke. Edwin's style was very different from his father's. Pastor Lakes Sr. was serious—an old-style-religion type. He was dignified and scholarly in his delivery, using big words and breaking down the Greek and Aramaic words in scripture.

Edwin was more down-to-earth. His style was simple, homey, and appealed to folks in the street because he didn't preach down to people. He made the Word understandable. He, too, knew the Greek and the Aramaic translations, but when he sprinkled that in he would also throw in a "Holla if ya hear me" every now and then, too. Faith Baptist had one of the youngest new memberships of any church in the city. Edwin was proud of his youth ministry because it meant something: It meant that people who might not ever get the Word of God were receiving it. They weren't waiting until they had one foot on a banana peel and the other foot planted in a grave. They were willing to change their lives early. They were the people that Edwin served.

"No, there will be no rock throwing today. We're going to talk truth. We're going to keep it very real today. Many years ago, before I even wanted to stand up here in front of this church and lead, I had a life. It wasn't a life I was looking for; it was a life that found me. Now, I'm not going to get all sanctimonious and talk about how 'the devil tempted me' and 'I was too weak,' because, while that may be true, it's not real. I wanted the life that found me. I enjoyed that life and that experience. And I wouldn't trade the experience for anything in the world."

More than a few gasps rose throughout the church, and a couple of mumbles could be heard near the back.

"Yes. I said I wouldn't trade that experience for anything in the world. Because that experience made me the pastor and the man I am today. I know temptation. I know what it is to fall. I know what it is to sin. I think it's important to know sin if you're going to serve the Lord. You have to know what you're dealing with. There's a reason why the police hire former thieves to help them crack a burglary ring. Sometimes you need a thief to catch a thief. It takes one to know one.

"Jesus may have been perfect, but none of his disciples were. The men Jesus chose to lead his church were all flawed, sin-filled individuals. Some were fishermen. But among them was a tax collector, one of the most vile people of Jesus' day. Among his flock was Mary, called Magdalene. In Luke, Chapter Eight, she is described as a woman from whom seven demons had emerged. Seven demons. A demon-possessed woman was one of his disciples!

"There is a book—a big bestseller—called *The Da Vinci Code*, that claims she was Jesus's wife and bore him children. Now, y'all know I don't believe any of that, but think about that for a minute. Jesus and Mary Magdalene were so close that people spread rumors about their relationship. And Jesus would still be Jesus if he were married, because last I looked that wasn't a sin. But the Bible does describe a close relationship between the two. She washed his feet with perfume before he was crucified. The point is, she was possessed by seven demons and Jesus chose her to be among his flock.

"Now, look around you. Who in here is without sin? And can any of your sins be worse than being possessed by *seven* demons?"

A few congregants nodded their head in agreement. And one man blurted, "No, pastor!"

"Can we even measure our sins against the next man's sins? I mean, who is to say that being an adulterer is better than being possessed by seven demons? Who is to say that being a thief is worse than being a liar? A sin is a sin. And only the Father in Heaven can judge any man on Earth. And when our Father came to Earth in the form of Jesus, he didn't judge. What did he do? Well, let's look at the Scripture. Turn to Verse Ten of John, Chapter Eight. Jesus told Mary Magdalene that he did not condemn her. He did not judge. He simply told her, 'Go now and leave your life of sin.'

"Now, I don't know about you, but I didn't come to the church a perfect man. Not even close. But once I left that life in Miami, Florida, I left my life of sin. I totally committed my life to Jesus. So I will not be judged. I will hold my head high because I have nothing to be ashamed of. I sinned. I repented. I was forgiven. Jesus died for all of that. That's the walk of a disciple of Christ."

A splattering of "Amen"s rose up throughout the church.

"This church my daddy built was a vision that I carried with me when I was called to step into the huge shoes he left for me to fill. I envisioned this as a temple of healing, where people learn the true Word and know the true meaning of being a disciple of God. It is not an easy walk. But if the journey is undertaken, it is completely fulfilling. I don't put a lot of stock in the pomp and circumstance of church. It's like 'playing church.' Now, don't get me wrong, I love the choir and Sister Jones, you sure do tear up those solos. It's like we have Patti LaBelle right here in our house. But that's not why we come to church, is it?

"We don't come to church to see who's wearing what or who's not wearing what. It's not to see who's driving what. And when you so-called celebrities show up, I can't give you preferential treatment, because you aren't special in the house of the Lord, you are just a disciple. God is not impressed by your celebrity status. There are no saved seats, because everyone has a seat in God's house. So if you all decide to keep me as your pastor—but it's not really your decision, but God's—I'm going to step it up. It's going to get a little more difficult. Some of us are going to be a little more uncomfortable with things. But that's good. Because that discomfort means there is growth. This church is not just going to increase in the number of people, it's going to grow in its spirit. That's a promise."

"Well, all right, now!" shouted Sister Jenkins, one of the deaconesses.

Edwin smiled, his first genuine smile of the day. He continued:

"Speaking of growth, I, too, have some areas of growth to work on. I will ask that you pray for me in these areas. I need my family back. I want you all to pray for Sister Patricia, so that she finds it in her heart to forgive me for not telling her about my past. And in that same vein, I want all of you to pray for Ritz Harper."

With that name, grumbles ripped through the sanctuary.

"What have I been talking about all morning? Don't condemn Ritz Harper! The walk with Christ is not easy. It is all about love. It's about forgiveness, not condemnation. It's about not holding grudges. How lost is that woman, that she has built her career spreading rumors about people, spreading vicious gossip, and destroying lives? How can she look herself in the mirror? How does she sleep at night?

"Yes, she's a millionaire, and many of you may think that she has everything. But the truth is, she has nothing.

"She needs our prayers right now—especially now, as she fights for her life. She needs to live so that she doesn't go to hell. And let me remind you, the primary goal of a follower of Christ is to make sure that people know the truth so that they can avoid Hell. So we are going to pray for Ritz Harper, and we are going to pray that she makes a full and speedy recovery. Then we are going to pray that she finds Christ. Someone in here may be the one to touch her. Someone in here might be the one to bring her into the light."

Tracee Remington sat in the fourth pew on the far right of the church. She hadn't come for the spectacle. She had come to hear the Word. She needed comfort. She didn't even know if Edwin Lakes would be preaching. Tracee just knew she had to be around believers. She had to stay plugged in. Reading her Bible wasn't enough. There was too much going on, and she had to be grounded. She bowed her head as Pastor Lakes instructed and she prayed as hard as she could for Ritz, her friend who had gained the world but lost her soul.

9

Ritz fought against that floating feeling. She knew that if she allowed herself to just go with the flow, it would be over. She knew that she would not, could not, return once she surrendered to that peaceful, tempting white light. If she followed her mother and left the place of limbo, she would be "officially dead." All that would be left of her would be a fancy funeral—which she would be in no condition to appreciate—and after the hoopla died down maybe every now and then there would be a few lines about her in David Hinckley's "Radio Dial" column in the *Daily News*. And her name wouldn't be in boldface type in that column.

The *News* did not boldface the names of dead people.

There was a part of her that wanted to give up, a part that wanted to just let go. What did she have waiting for her back there? She didn't have a man. There was a career that was booming, but it took all her energy to keep it hot, and that career did not make her happy, though she tried to convince herself that it did. She felt so bad for herself.

Ritz tried to process everything her mother had said to her and it added up to one thing: She was a bad person. She had no friends except for Tracee, and Tracee had changed so much. She wondered who Tracee really was now.

Despite the temptations of that bright light, Ritz had a burning desire to come back. She wanted to live. She had things she needed to take care of. At the top of her list was revenge. Ritz wanted to get whoever shot her. She wanted to live so she could get them. They say that living well is the best revenge. No, revenge is the best revenge.

The Sicilians have a saying: "Revenge is a dish best served cold." Ritz once heard somebody on *The Sopranos* say that. At the time, she didn't know what those words meant. But now she did.

It would all come later. Let the dish get cold. Right now, she had something else to do.

She reached deep inside herself to that place in her heart that made her special, the place that made her strong, the place that was Ritgina "Ritz" Harper.

Live. Live. Live. Breathe. Breathe. Breathe.

She felt a tingly sensation that seemed to be a mile down south. Then she realized: Those were her toes. She wiggled them.

Then she felt another tingly sensation—coming from her left and from her right.

They were her arms. She could feel them. Then she felt her hands coming back.

Could she give someone the finger?

She tried, and she could feel the middle finger of her right hand rising.

Yes!

Then she could feel that she was on her back and that all kinds of things were stuck in her body. They hurt. She could hear an air conditioner humming. She could feel a harsh light on her eyelids. She could make out faint voices; she couldn't understand what they were saying, but the voices were getting clearer and clearer. Her left butt cheek itched. She ran her tongue along her teeth. They were still there.

Ritz tried to talk, but there were tubes stuck in her mouth.

"Thank you, Mama. I love you, Mama." That's what she was trying to say.

☆ ★ ☆

"Doctor, come quick! I think Ritz Harper is coming out of her coma!" said the nurse who was on duty.

Paul Grevious was at the nurses' station. He had just checked on his most famous patient and was going to finish his rounds. There was a lot of attention around this case, and Dr. Grevious was taking his time to make sure he didn't make a single mistake. This case could make his career. He was a solid neurosurgeon, but he wanted to be known as the best.

This case had already brought him the first press conference he had ever done. That was the night after Ritz Harper was identified. He didn't have much to report other than that she was in critical condition and in a coma.

There would be many more press conferences if she held on, and lived, and was able to discuss her "progress" with a tabloid press that would pant like a puppy dog after his every word.

And if he played his cards right, Dr. Grevious figured, there might even be a book deal in the mix somewhere. He was going to make sure that Ritz Harper got the best care possible, and he was also going to make sure that everyone knew who provided that care.

When his beeper went off, Dr. Grevious raced to Ritz's room. Lights! Camera! Action!

Ritz's eyes were fluttering. The pace on the heart monitor was quickening. She seemed to be moving her lips. Finally, she opened her eyes.

"Welcome back, stranger," Dr. Grevious said, smiling. He took out his light and checked her pupils. There was still some swelling around her eyes, so he was very gentle. Ritz tried to talk, but it was painful. It felt like she had swallowed a bunch of chopped glass. The tube they had shoved down her throat to feed her had made her throat raw. Her eyes hurt. Her head was pounding. She couldn't take a deep breath without feeling a stabbing pain. The grimace that was etched across her face told the story.

"Nurse, get Ms. Harper some morphine, stat!" Dr. Grevious

said. He smiled at Ritz. "The worst part is over, Ms. Harper. We're going to focus now on getting you back on your feet."

Ritz opened her eyes. Her vision was blurry and she felt pain all around the sockets. Her head pounded, as if the entire cast from *Drumline* were practicing in her head: *Rat-a-tat-tat!* Her chest hurt, her knees hurt, her side hurt. She was a bundle of pain.

Tears streaked down the sides of her face, creating another kind of hot pain that started from somewhere inside. The great Ritz Harper, the "Queen of All Media," was flat on her back and helpless. Ritz prided herself on her independence. Since her mother died, she had lived as if she could rely on no one but herself.

At the tender age of ten, Ritz decided she was going to take care of herself. She appreciated her aunt and uncle for raising her, giving her a home, and loving her, but Ritz never relied on them. She always had odd jobs as a kid. She sold flowers in the neighborhood, flowers she plucked from her aunt's garden. She did chores for a fee. Ritz wasn't afraid of work. And she saved every penny. She was not miserly, but she was afraid—afraid of being alone and helpless. While outsiders didn't understand the method to her madness, Ritz knew exactly what she was doing when she would pay cash for her car and try to pay off her home as quickly as possible. Financial advisors told her that what she was doing was stupid, that you spend other people's money, that loans are your friends. To Ritz, a loan was a dependency on somebody else, and that didn't work for her. If something happened, they

WENDY WILLIAMS *and* KAREN HUNTER ☆ *71*

could come and take her car or take her home and she would be left with nothing. She wanted to own her stuff—outright. She didn't want anyone to be able to take anything from her—not even her life. She fought hard every day to live, because she wanted whoever had the audacity to try and take her life to feel her wrath.

To Ritz, life was all about power and control. She wanted the power and she wanted the control. Power and control were her twin babies, and she would give those babies to no one—not for one minute, not for one second.

And now she was laid up in a hospital bed, completely powerless with zero control. She couldn't even take herself to the bathroom. Her most humiliating experience was the day she soiled her sheets and two orderlies had to come in and literally lift her from her bed while the nurse cleaned the bed, changed her sheets, and washed her.

Ritz was screaming inside. She was Ritz Fucking Harper, not some damn invalid who had to have her ass wiped by someone. But at the moment, she *was* an invalid who had to have her ass wiped for her.

Some of the nurses were surly. Ritz was given the deluxe star treatment, complete with a private room and other amenities that were found more at the Ritz-Carlton than in a hospital. But the staff was still the hospital staff. Ritz had four nurses who worked eight-hour shifts. Two of them were nice, but two acted like they did not want to be there. They treated her like they hated her. One was so rude that, if Ritz had any strength whatsoever, she would have slapped her.

But she could barely move, let alone haul off and slap someone. She was completely at everyone's mercy. Her biggest nightmare was what happened to the Uma Thurman charac- ter in *Kill Bill* when she was in a coma and one of the hospi- tal workers charged a fee for men to have their way with her while she was unconscious. Ritz didn't even want to think about what could have happened to her while she was in a coma and totally helpless.

Ritz hadn't processed yet that she was under constant watch and guard. She hadn't even thought about the killer possibly trying again. Her only thought was getting back. She wanted to get back on top as quickly as possible.

In a way, she was in her element in the hospital. Hospitals were for folks who were in pain, and Ritz had spent almost her whole life in pain. So, in the hospital, Ritz felt very much at home.

The door to Ritz Harper's private room opened. Ritz opened her eyes to see Aunt Madalyn and Uncle Cecil.

"Hey, baby girl," Uncle Cecil said. He stroked her hand, which had an IV tube in it.

Ritz managed to croak out a "Hey." She didn't expect to feel what she was feeling. Red shame spread across her chest when she looked at Cecil and then to Madalyn, who looked so old and worn. It seemed as though twenty years had passed since she last saw her aunt and uncle, instead of only a year.

The reason why they hadn't spoken in that time was so petty, Ritz now knew. Her aunt was disappointed in her behavior, and her aunt had been right.

Ritz had been too caught up in her rise in the game to have any naysaying or negative feedback thrown in her face. She felt like her aunt didn't understand her ambition, and therefore she wasn't going to speak to her until Ritz got exactly what she wanted, which was to be told that she was right. Then Ritz would say, "See, I told you so."

But she didn't feel much like saying that now. Ritz remembered the words her mother had spoken to her, and those words had cut her deep. She remembered the last nasty words she said to her aunt: "That's some bullshit to go along with your slave mentality. You didn't raise me. My mother raised me, and she didn't raise a slave!"

"Slave mentality." Her Auntie M was the most liberated person Ritz had ever known. Auntie M was naturally beautiful. Auntie M was brilliant. Auntie M had a man whom she loved and who loved her. Auntie M's life had a purpose and a joy. Auntie M had raised her, without complaint, with unconditional love.

Auntie M didn't need a boob job, and a manicured twat, and a thousand-dollar wig, and a big fur coat, and a million dollars in the bank, to make herself feel "free." Auntie M *was* free—she always had been, and always would be.

So who, in fact, was really the "slave"? Who, underneath all the makeup, and the bling, and the money, was the one who truly had the "slave mentality"?

Ritz shut her eyes to try to hold in the tears. They were streaming down the sides of her face anyway. Aunt Madalyn stood by Cecil's side as he put his arm around her, practically holding her up.

"I'm so sorry," Ritz squeaked out. "I'm sorry, Auntie M.

Please forgive me." The tears now flowed steadily. It was like a cork had been popped on a bottle of champagne.

Madalyn managed a smile and squeezed Ritz's hand, which seemed to be the only part of her body not bandaged.

"I'm sorry, too, baby. I love you."

Ritz nodded and squeezed her aunt's hand. And at that moment, she knew that she was going to be all right.

I'm sorry, too, baby. I love you.

Who said that? Was it Auntie M or was it Mama? Or both?

Later that night, for the first time since she was a little child, Ritgina Harper fell asleep with a smile on her face.

11

Delilah Summers smoothed the skirt of her blue, pin-striped Brooks Brothers suit. She hadn't worn that suit or any other suit in nearly a year. It was a little snug around the hips and waist, but she could mask that well. Television people are masters of illusion. They know how to hide a few extra pounds, a new wrinkle, or newly sprouted grays. They had tricks— from how to stand and sit to hide a bulge (angle your body sideways and thrust your chest forward), to the special Der-mablend cover-up makeup, to the little magic coloring stick when there isn't time to get to the salon for a color treatment.

And there was always Miss Clairol when the job was big-ger than a little covering around the temples. Delilah was a pro. She'd been there, done that, many, many times.

All she thought about was getting back on television (and, of course, getting back at Ritz Harper). She knew her day would come, that she would get back to the top. She just never expected to have to basically start from scratch.

"Screen test?!" Delilah howled into the phone when her agent, Frank Baker from the William Morris Agency, told her about the newsmagazine show CNN was launching.

"I am Delilah Summers! Don't they know what I can do already? Doesn't *everybody* know what I can do?!"

"You *were* Delilah Summers," said Frank, who never bit his tongue and never tried to soften the truth with one of his most difficult and most famous clients. "CNN knows what you used to be. But quite frankly, Delilah, few people come back from scandal."

"Pat O'Brien came back!"

"Pat O'Brien is in *entertainment*," Frank said. "That's fluff. They thrive on scandal in entertainment. Hell, that probably helped his career. You are a *news*woman—a serious newswoman. Look what happened to Dan Rather. He left the business in shame. They didn't give a damn that he worked more than forty years bringing the truth at a high level. They didn't care that he risked his life covering wars. They didn't care about his stellar record. He has one bad spill and bam! It's over. Hasta la vista! You're basically starting all over again, Delilah."

"That bitch!" Delilah muttered under her breath, barely audible.

"I'm sorry, Delilah," Frank said. "Let's just knock 'em out, show them that you're ready—that the rumors of your weight gain and mental deterioration are just rumor."

Delilah tightened her jaw. She couldn't believe that all that she had worked for over so many years could be so frivolously tossed aside. Delilah wasn't completely discouraged. She was still relatively young. Katie Couric, who became the first woman to anchor the *CBS Evening News,* was fifty and still considered a youngster. Diane Sawyer was over sixty and Barbara Walters, hell, she went to high school with Methuselah. Delilah was younger than the youngest by more than a decade. Time was on her side to re-create herself and make a serious comeback. But this comeback had to be for good.

She still couldn't grasp that Ritz Harper—that no-talent lackey, as she referred to her—could not only bring her down in one fell swoop, but could then go on to become one of the biggest names out there.

That bitch!

That had become Delilah's mantra.

"I am not going out like that!" Delilah declared to Frank. "I will be back!"

"Of course you will," he said. "That's why we never dropped you. I knew it was just a matter of time. Now, get your fanny in gear. You cannot be late!"

12

Jacob Reese's cell phone rang. He was nervous about answering it. He saw the news reports that said Ritz Harper was still alive. He was all dressed up with nowhere to go. He had on his go-get-my-money suit and just hours ago he was buying buildings and building his personal empire. Now everything was in jeopardy.

Jacob fidgeted as he answered the phone.

"Hello?"

"The bitch is not dead!" The voice on the other end spit the words out. "You fucked up. You don't get your dough until you finish the job." *Click*.

Jacob was fuming. He knew he wasn't cut out to be a hit man. It seemed like he couldn't do anything right. He had big dreams but no follow-through or execution. He had a failed marriage that was his fault because he kept coming up with these get-rich-quick schemes and squandering the family's hard-earned money. His wife finally got fed up.

"You can break yourself, but I work too damn hard to go broke," she'd said before she left. He realized that love didn't conquer all, money did. He had dreams that his wife would come back once he got himself together. But she had moved on.

He couldn't hold a steady job, because he never focused on doing the job he was paid to do. He came into the workplace like he was doing them a favor showing up every day. And Jacob spent his time at his job on the company phone, setting studio times, trying to make deals with producers, and working to get his demos heard. He was wheeling and dealing, and eventually he ended up being wheeled right out of the job.

His music career went nowhere, and now this had been his big chance to get paid—or at least give him a leg up on really getting paid—and he couldn't get that right, either.

"How did that fucking bitch live?" he said. "I know I had to get one of those bullets near her heart. Shit! Shit! Shit!"

He got in his car and drove to the hospital. He figured he could slip in there and maybe smother her and finish the job. He'd seen that done a couple of times on television. But the hospital was teeming with police and security. He decided he would lay low, strike when they least expected it.

"I'll have another opportunity. The next time she will die."

13

Chas saw no reason to call the rest of Ritz's crew to the meeting. Aaron and Jamie would have to go along with whatever plan Chas hatched if they wanted to continue to work for the Ritz Harper Excursion.

Chas had one phone call to make before he went to meet with Ernest Ruffin about his replacement for Ritz. Moon was a radio personality who had been run out of every town he worked in because of something he said that was controversial. After the death of rap superstar Notorious B.I.G., he played the sound effects of a gun and then a cow mooing and said, "Got beef? Well, believe me, sweetie, we now have enough to feed the needy. Good riddance to that fat ass." That didn't sit well with the folks in Connecticut, where Moon's morning show was always in the top three. The calls that came in following that forced the station to suspend him indefinitely. He landed in South Carolina, where some comments about "crackers" and "rednecks" got him another pink slip. At his next gig, he had a beef with a rival jock in Ohio and threatened to kidnap his daughter and shave her head. He said he was joking, but folks don't take kindly to threats made against four-year-old girls. But in radio folks seem to have a short memory. So now he had the top-rated show in the nation's capital.

Chas had had his eye on Moon for a while. Actually, he had his hands on him at one time. The two were fuck buddies who'd met at one of those exclusive clubs. Chas instantly liked how raw he was. Moon was a high school dropout, an undercover brother. He hid his sexuality behind rugged B-boy clothes and a nasty disposition. He came off tough and mean and could verbally abuse someone to tears. Moon's insecurities over being found out as gay and his lack of education made him even more ferocious. He was a voracious reader. He wanted to make sure that no one could challenge him intellectually. He had ready-made comebacks for anyone who came at him. His philosophy was to hit someone so hard that they didn't think about coming back. And it worked.

Chas cut right through all of that bravado and BS. Moon loved that Chas could see the real him. He was sprung. Chas always left a man feeling like a king, even if he was only going to be a king for the night. Moon was one of those who wanted to be a king forever. But that could never happen. Chas wasn't the "forever" type. Besides, Moon was too insecure for Chas to have so much control over him in a relationship. Moon was a classic loose cannon that could blow at any time. Chas needed his man to be predictable.

Moon's volatile personality, however, made for fabulous radio. The great thing about him was that while people hated him, they *loved* to hate him. There is regular hate where people are repulsed, and then there is hate that brings intrigue and is addictive. It's why so many people stay in bad relationships. They know they need to leave that abusive man or cheating woman, but they can't because they believe the next time it will be different.

But it never is. The abuser or cheat is so charming that they promise never to do it again, and they are believed every time. And every single time they are lying. Moon was one of those types. He was a perfect replacement for Ritz.

Chas had Aaron compile two weeks' worth of *Best of* shows featuring some of Ritz's interviews, including her final interview with Ivan Richardson, the man who had outed one of the hottest ministers in the country. That one they repeated twice during the packaged shows.

Chas needed to secure one more thing before he met with the bosses at WHOT.

"Moon?"

"Yo, whassup? Who this?"

"It's Chas. I don't have a lot of time to go into details, but I need to know if you're up to leaving that rinky-dink station of yours in D.C. and head back to New York for your chance at the big time?"

"Rinky-dink? Nigga, I'm in the nation's capital and I'm numero uno. Please! For what station?"

"Stop smelling yourself. I need to know if you're interested," Chas said.

"I'm listening. What you got?"

"I'll call you back with the details," Chas said, and hung up before Moon could respond. Chas didn't want to have too much conversation. He was a student of the 48 Laws of Power. And Law No. 4: Always Say Less Than Necessary, implied, "Powerful people impress and intimidate by saying less." Chas had mastered that. He had mastered quite a few of the laws, including Law No. 8: Make Other People Come to You—Use Bait if Necessary. He loved being around hungry people and holding all the food.

Moon was very hungry.

Now was the time for Chas to see how well he'd studied the laws of power. If he could pull off this coup at WHOT, he would be the official master.

Chas drove up Park Avenue and was rounding the block to the garage that he normally parked in near the station.

"What a difference a couple of days makes," he said.

It was only a few days earlier that Chas had been on this same street and all was calm. It had just been another day, with people going to and from work. Today there were some leftover pieces of yellow police tape, and reporters and news trucks parked out front. Undercover detectives were surveying the area and interviewing anyone who may have seen anything. They were looking for any lead that might uncover who had shot Ritz Harper.

Chas pulled into the garage. He got the ticket and handed his keys to the attendant. He smoothed out his silk shirt and let his hands run down his linen-blend pants. He walked past the reporters and the police, took a deep breath, and pushed through the revolving door.

He was about to employ Laws No. 28 and 29: "Enter Action with Boldness" and "Plan All the Way to the End."

If it worked to perfection, Chas would knock the queen out of the box and be the undisputed king of all media.

14

"I don't give a fuck!" Ritz's voice was very hoarse and crackly from lack of use. It was also raw from the tubes—which had been removed just two days before—that had been running down her throat and into her stomach, feeding her for the weeks that she was in a coma. The intent and delivery, however, were still very Ritz Harper–like—all diva.

Ritz's recovery was going well. She had a lot of time to lie in bed and think about everything that had happened. She was getting antsy. She wanted to get back in the game. Ritz needed to be back on the air.

Since coming out of the coma, she was feeling stronger every day. She could finally take herself to the bathroom. Her wounds were healing nicely. Her collapsed lung, which was reinflated, was also healing well, although the doctor suggested that she do no loud talking. Ritz was not a very good patient.

"You get Chas on the phone right now! I am going back on the air tomorrow!" she yelled.

"But, Miss Harper, you don't understand. You were shot," said Dr. Grevious. "You lost a lot of blood. You almost died. You're still very weak."

"Muthafucker, I *know* I was shot! If anyone knows I was shot, it's me! And the only weak thing in this room is standing in front of me telling me what I'm not going to do," Ritz said. "If you can't do what I ask, I want another doctor. And you better bring a hospital engineer in here, too. I need an ISDN line hooked up immediately. And give me some more painkillers. Now!"

The ISDN line would enable Ritz to have broadcast-quality sound. It would be a direct feed into the studio's equipment. Ritz had an ISDN line hooked up in her home, just in case she needed to do her show from home, which was rare. There were many on-air personalities who frequently did their show from their homes. Rush Limbaugh's home was his studio. Doug Stephens, a syndicated morning talk-show host, had several homes throughout the country from which he broadcast. It was actually rare for him to do a show from the studio. It would seem like a dream for most to be able to roll out of bed or from wherever and for four hours work from the comforts of their home. That was the life. But Ritz chose to go in every day. It made her show feel and sound more authentic.

Besides, she had live guests and she didn't want any of those people knowing where she lived. Ritz's show was unique. It demanded that she be in New York, in the studio, in the mix of everything.

Ritz preferred it that way. She loved the commute in from New Jersey, especially on days when she was driven. She felt like a real celebrity in the tinted Lincoln Town Car or the Navigator that the station paid to have her driven in every day. She loved being on Park Avenue, where the wealthy lived and did their shopping. It was quintessentially everything Ritz had imagined about working in New York—walking into the hi-rise, hi-tech Park Avenue address, decked out in the latest designer gear and frames, looking fabulous. No one could see you if you worked from home. You couldn't be admired or even hated from your home. You couldn't be a star working from your home. Ritz wanted stardom, and that meant coming into the city every day, being seen, and doing her job better than anybody else.

She also loved interacting with the people at WHOT. She wasn't friendly with anyone there. She mostly barked orders or received praise. But the interaction made her feel like somebody. And that was important to Ritz Harper.

"Miss Harper, we have a package for you" was the greeting she got every afternoon when she arrived, always two hours early, for her shift. She loved the packages from some fan or public relations person trying to butter her up to be nice to their client.

"Miss Harper, Eduard Davis just sent you a box of his latest designs!"

Eduard's couture shirt company was called Karma, with the tag "Looking Good Is the Best Revenge." Ritz loved the Urban Hippie line of Karma, which was ironic because she never quite grasped the concept of karma in her own life.

"Miss Harper, Don Ramos called. He has a necklace that he made for you to wear at the awards program next week."

Years ago, it was Jakob the Jeweler who was Ritz's jewelry person, but he got too famous and too big. That was before the money-laundering scandal that got him arrested and on the front pages of the local papers. Until that point, everybody who was anybody in entertainment had visited and purchased from Jakob the Jeweler. Ritz dumped him long before the controversy. He became too common. She found Don Ramos—actually, he found her—before she was even big enough to afford the jewels. He saw Ritz's potential. So she gave him a shout-out every chance she got on the air. In exchange, she got thousands of dollars of free diamonds and platinum jewelry—one of the many perks of being Ritz Harper. She loved the perks. She loved being big enough to make other people successful, too.

Being a star was what Ritz Harper lived for. Being in a hospital bed, with tubes sticking out of her, an ugly hospital gown with her ass out, no makeup, no hairpieces or wigs—for crying out loud, it was a bit more than she could take. She had to get back. And she had to get back now.

She pressed the emergency button to call for the nurse.

Her second-shift nurse came running in. She was one of the nice ones. This was the first encounter any of the nursing staff would have with a fully awake, almost full-strength Ritz Harper.

"Yes, Miss Harper?" said Nurse Betty-Jean. "What can I get you?"

"You can start by telling me where my shit is." Ritz hadn't thought about her personal effects until now.

"Um, you didn't come in with anything—not even ID."

"What?! Where is my fifteen-thousand-dollar Gucci crocodile bag?! Where is my cell phone? Where is my makeup?!"

"Like I said, Miss Harper, you only came in with the clothes on your back. I'm sorry."

"You certainly are! How do I get an outside line on this phone?"

"Just dial nine and there will be a dial tone, and dial whatever number you need to. Is there anything else I can get you? Do you need some water or something?"

"I asked that doctor for some more painkillers," Ritz said. "Do you think you can make that happen?"

"I have to consult with your doctor first. But I'm sure that won't be a problem. I'll be right back."

Ritz took a deep breath. It hurt to breathe. She must have irritated her lung with all of that yelling. Then everything started to hurt. The pain medication had definitely worn off, and reality hit Ritz. Her head was pounding. Her eye socket was throbbing, too. And there was a rumble of pain in her chest. She grabbed her breast and noticed that it was flat. "What the fuck?!"

Ritz had not taken inventory of her injuries. It had been less than two weeks since she had come out of the coma. She knew she had been shot. But she had been so caught up in her emotions that she wasn't thinking about her physical state. From seeing her mother, whether it was for real or in a dream, to reuniting with her aunt and knowing that they still had things to work out, to reconciling with the fact that someone actually tried to kill her—Ritz was an emotional wreck. She knew she had to "recover," but what that entailed, she had no clue.

She pulled back her gown to see the heavy bandages and a drain in her breast area. One of her plump, perfectly implanted breasts was now flat as a pancake. She hadn't looked in the mirror, either. If she had, the sight of her swollen, bandaged face and black eye would have been enough for her to forget about her plans of leaving the hospital. She would not have wanted any photos taken of her in this condition, and there were paparazzi camping out, hoping for an opportunity to snap a shot of Ritz Harper.

"Maybe the doctor is right. Maybe I'm not ready," she said to herself. Then, just as quickly, she shook the thought out. "I have to come back. That motherfucker who did this to me is not getting away with this. I have to show everyone that I will be back and better than ever. Now, where the fuck is Chas?"

Chas had not been back to the hospital since that first

night. Ritz really missed him and was confused by his absence.

"What's all the noise and commotion? You have the nurses' station all in a tizzy. Behave yourself!" said Tracee, as she walked into Ritz's room.

"Hey, lady," Ritz said. "Where's Chas?"

"I don't know. I haven't seen him for a minute."

"How long have you been here?"

"Since you stood me up at the airport. You know how I hate to wait at the airport!" Tracee said, trying to get Ritz to lighten up.

This was the first time the two friends had actually gotten to talk alone—there was always someone in the room. Tracee kept a low profile. She wanted to give Ritz time to heal. She was also well aware that the shooter was still out there and she wanted to keep everything around Ritz calm and normal—as close to normal as possible under the circumstances.

Tracee had been there. She had spent every waking hour of the last two weeks at the hospital, at Ritz's bedside, with her aunt and uncle, with the detectives. She was the rock, holding everything together, keeping their spirits up.

"I know, I know," Ritz said. "Believe me, it wasn't my fault. Can you please get Chas on the phone for me? I need to see about getting an ISDN hookup in this hospital."

"For what?!" Tracee looked incredulous.

"Tracee, if I don't go right back, I'm not sure if I ever will," she said. "I have to show the motherfucker who did this that he can't kill me. I'm still here. I need people to know that."

"You aren't even allowed to have a cell phone in here—why would you contemplate a radio show? I think that coma ruined some brain cells, too!"

"You don't understand, Tray. I have to get back. I have to get back on the air as soon as possible. I have to!"

"The only thing you *have* to do right now is stay black and keep living. Your ass almost died. Oh, wait a minute. You *did* die. I was holding your hand when you flatlined. I was pushed out of the room when the nurses and doctors came in with the defibrillator to bring you back. I was here with your aunt and uncle, crying for days when you wouldn't wake up. I remember every moment. That radio will be there. Or maybe it won't. But you, Ritz, you have to take care of yourself."

"But you don't understand!" Ritz shouted. "I—"

"Oh, hell no! You aren't going to yell at me. I'm not one of your peons. And you're supposed to keep your voice down. You're constantly going, trying to hit the next mark. Maybe this happened for a reason. Maybe you got slowed down because God is trying to get your attention."

"Don't bring God into this. I'm halfway thinking that this God of yours ain't all he's cracked up to be," Ritz said.

"Watch your mouth! That God of mine is the reason why you're still breathing. You better know that what happened to you didn't just happen."

"Not you, too!" Ritz said.

"What? What are you talking about?"

"Nothing. So you're saying it's my fault I got shot?"

"No, I'm saying it's your fault that you aren't paying attention to what's happening to yourself and the world around you. It's your fault that you're so caught up in your own ambition that you've forgotten how to treat people. It's your fault that you spend so much time working on your outside and how you look that you haven't done much work on your inside, building your spirit."

Ritz was stung by Tracee's words.

"Why are you coming down on me?" Ritz said. "I was the one who was fucking shot by some fucking nut job. Somebody tried to fucking kill me! I don't give a fuck what I did in the past, I've never done anything to warrant that!"

"You're not hearing me. Of course you didn't do anything to warrant being shot. I'm just saying you should take this time and use it as an opportunity for self-reflection. Use it as a catalyst to make some changes."

"Yeah, I am going to make some changes. The first one is to fire Chas if his ass doesn't come here real soon and let me know what he's doing to get me back on the air."

Tracee could see that Ritz wasn't ready to have a deep conversation. She backed off. Another time would come. Tracee didn't want to upset her friend, she wanted her to get better and heal. But she wanted some healing to come from within, too.

"I'll call him right now," Tracee said. "You just relax. I overheard the nurse saying she had to bring you some painkillers. That should put you out for a minute. Sleep and take care of yourself. I will be right here. I'm not going anywhere."

Chas wanted a sober assessment of what he thought was a perfect night. He gently pulled back the covers, and the sun was literally shining on what he believed to be the perfect ass. It was full, tight, perfectly round, with dimples on either side.

Positively delicious, Chas thought. Just looking at it made Chas want to sink his teeth into it. He knew he would have to have a taste before he left. Chas loved one-night stands. He loved the cat-and-mouse chase in the first moments, when his eyes locked on his prey at a club, the instant electricity, and the tight pull on his loins that let him know there was indeed a connection. He loved the quickened pace and pounding of his heart in anticipation of that first kiss. The urgency of getting somewhere to release all of the sexual tension that was building up was the most exciting. It could be in a dark corner of a park, in an alleyway, in a car. The unfolding mystery of where he would actually find sexual grati-fication made the chase more like a drug. He had to have it. He always had to do it with someone new.

Chas couldn't remember the last relationship he had. It was probably high school, when the thought of being with somebody for an extended time was part of the fantasy of life. Having that special someone who was your very own, who would be there forever. But when he walked in on his special someone going down on the star quarterback, Chas's fantasies were dashed. The reality was, there was no such thing as hap-pily ever after—at least not forever. There was only happily right now, until the next new thing came along.

He used men just like he used everyone for his own pur-poses. Mr. Perfect Ass's purpose this night was just to allow Chas to release some tension. Chas's plans of bringing Moon to New York were dashed. Ernest Ruffin had other plans, and it included bringing Ritz back as soon as she was able. The news was getting around quickly that Ritz was recovering. Ruff asked him to extend her *Best of* shows for one more week and then they would have guest hosts fill in for one week at a time. Chas was trying to work Moon in as one of the fill-ins, but Ruff wanted to keep the female flavor flowing.

"You know the female audience is one of the most coveted in radio. Ritz has been able to dominate that market. I don't want to mess with that," he said. "We're going to put some placeholders in there until Miss Ritz is ready to regain her spot."

Ruff's decision made Chas boil inside. That was not his

plan. Chas's plan included replacing Ritz altogether and showing that he was the actual mastermind behind the success of the Excursion. He could create a star out of anyone, and if he got the chance to put Moon on the air, he would prove it. But Chas had to play it cool. He had created Ritz just as Dr. Frankenstein had created that thing, that monster. And now all eyes were on Dr. Chas's Miss Thing. What an unlucky break, he thought, that she was recovering.

A fake smile crossed Chas's face as Ruff was speaking.

"So I need your help in shaping these shows over the next few weeks and bringing in some hot guests," Ruff continued. "Do I have your cooperation?"

"Of course," Chas said. "The only reason why I brought up Moon was because I didn't want Ritz's ratings to drop even one point. And I knew that Moon could stir enough shit to keep WHOT hot. But your plan makes perfect sense. So who's the first fill-in?"

"Michelle Davis."

"That hot chick from Fox?" Chas said. Chas might be gay, but he wasn't blind. She did not have a face for radio. She had a face for television. And if she could bring any of that hotness over the airwaves, he may be able to stick to his plan, just shift it from a Moon to a real star.

"Yep, that's the one," Ruff said. "She's excited about doing it. She doesn't normally do radio, but she said she really hit it off with Ritz when she interviewed her for that magazine piece and had her on her weekend talk show on Fox. She considers it an honor."

"Well, I consider it an honor working with her," said Chas.

Chas went to the club that evening and picked up Mr. Perfect Ass. He went to Mr. Perfect Ass's place—appropriately, in the Meatpacking District of New York. Chas did his best plotting while he was plowing into some fresh meat. He was often mistaken for a bottom, the kind of man who liked to take it because of his slight build and elegant ways. But Chas was a top dog all the way.

He walked over to the world's best ass and rubbed his hand across the round, smooth surface—the result of fresh waxing. Chas aroused himself quicker than even he could believe. He reached over and grabbed a condom off the end table and put it on. Mr. Perfect Ass stirred. Chas climbed on top of him, straddling that ass. He grabbed his hips and guided him upward as Chas reached around to feel Mr. Perfect Ass's equally perfect penis, which was completely swollen. Mr. Perfect Ass let out a moan in anticipation as Chas parted the man's cheeks with his other hand and carefully guided his own fully engorged penis into the opening. Chas slowly tapped once and then expertly found his spot as he leaned forward, letting himself fall in with an exhilarating thrust.

While he was grinding and churning himself into a frenzy, Chas thought how good it felt being top dog. He thought about everything he had accomplished. He thought about Ritz, and with a guttural moan, he exploded. Chas fell off and onto his back, chest heaving as Mr. Perfect Ass removed his condom and massaged his spent private parts.

Chas was deep in thought. He thought about the shooting.

He thought about his next move. He had a lot of business to tie up. He knew what needed to happen, but he had to make sure that he and the program director, Ernest Ruffin, were on the same page.

Chas slid out of bed and walked, still deep in thought, to the bathroom. Stopping in his tracks, Chas put his arms out, touching both walls in the hallway leading to the bathroom. He turned and said matter-of-factly, "I got a lot on my mind, so I'm gonna let myself out after I shower. I'll call you."

Chas had no intentions of calling. He was too engrossed in the other things that were turning him on lately. The power tripping. The puppeteering. The masterminding. He had a plan. And if it worked, no piece of ass could top the feeling that would be awaiting him.

16

Randolph Jordan was satisfied. He had finally landed a big contract that would pay him six figures for about three weeks of work. He was set to rewire a hospital on the East Side. Since leaving corporate America and starting his own electrical contracting business, Randolph wasn't sure if he'd made the right choice. The first couple of years were lean, to say the least. But business was certainly picking up.

The two men he had hired to help him with the job met him in the hospital lobby. It was unusually busy, he thought, with a lot of people who looked neither sick nor like medical staff.

"What's the commotion about?" he asked the security guard at the front desk of the hospital. Everyone had to sign in and show ID. Security was extra strict.

"Ritz Harper is a patient here, and those people over there

are reporters trying to catch a scoop," he said, pointing to the ragtag team stationed in the emergency room waiting area. "Over there are plainclothes cops. They're checking every single person who comes in. Whoever shot Ritz Harper is still out there."

"Ritz Harper?" Randolph said, looking puzzled. He hadn't really followed the news or gossip pages. He had read somewhere that the radio shock jock had been shot, but he had no idea she would be in the very hospital he'd be working in.

"Yeah, that bitch on the radio who's always gossiping about someone," the guard said. "Someone tried to put her out of her misery, I guess."

Randolph didn't respond. He was in a daze. He flashed back to the very memorable evening he spent with Ritz Harper and how he really did have to take a cold shower when he got home. She left quite an impression. He expected to see her again. He just never expected it would be like this.

Randolph had a brief meeting with his men and showed them exactly what they would be working on for the day. Ironically, their work zone was on the same floor as Ritz Harper. Randolph took the opportunity to stop in and see her. There was a guard standing in the outer area. He showed him his contractor's ID and told him that he was a friend.

He put his electrical-tool belt down and walked in. The hospital had set up a mini waiting area in the room next to Ritz's room. He hesitantly poked his head into the room. His eyes locked with Tracee's and he could have sworn he saw her blush.

"Hi, I . . . I don't mean to disturb you all, but I just wanted to stop by and see how Miss Harper was doing," Randolph said. "How is she?"

Tracee was sitting in front of the door and Madalyn and Cecil were next to her. Ritz was sleeping. They were all waiting for the doctor to come by and give them some news of her condition.

"We don't know much," said Tracee, who smiled for the first time in a week. "She's out of the coma, but she isn't completely out of the woods. But she thinks she is, which is a good thing. Ritz has a lot of fight in her."

"What did you say your name was?" Aunt Madalyn said.

"Oh, I'm sorry, ma'am, my name is Randolph, Randolph Jordan," he said. "I fixed Miss Harper's Jacuzzi a couple of months ago. She's quite a lady. I hope she has a complete recovery. I started listening to her on the radio and I miss her. I just wanted to come by and pay my respects."

"Okay, we'll tell her you stopped by when she wakes up," said Aunt Madalyn.

"I'll be around for a while. I just got a contract to do some wiring on this floor in the hospital," he said. "So if it's okay, I'd like to stop by tomorrow."

"Of course you can," said Aunt Madalyn.

"Thank you," Randolph said. "I'm going to get back to my work. I look forward to seeing you all tomorrow."

"Okay," Madalyn and Cecil said in unison.

The pleasure will be all mine, Tracee was thinking. She felt very naughty. But what she said was "See you tomorrow."

Randolph smiled at Tracee as he left.

"And he has the nerve to have dimples, too," Tracee said to herself.

It had been more than a year since she had a relationship. When she left New York, she left everything, including the boyfriend she had been seeing for three years. Her life had been superficial. She had the high-profile job as a record company executive. She had the perfect Manhattan loft and the perfect investment banker boyfriend. He was Jack-and-Jill, Alpha Phi Alpha, 100 Black Men perfect. He was bring-home-for-Thanksgiving and fit-right-in-with-the-family perfect. He was there for the Grammys, American Music Awards, the BET Awards. He wore Brooks Brothers and Armani, spectacles, and had perfect diction. He would have made the perfect husband and the perfect father. Had Tracee stayed around, they would have had a house in the Hamptons or Sag Harbor and two-point-five children within four years.

One snag. This man didn't believe in God. When Tracee started going to church, he refused, saying, "Please don't get too caught up in that holy-roller stuff, Tracee." The more Tracee got caught up, the more she started reading her Bible and studying the Word, the more she realized that she was leading a shallow life. Her life was all about the appearances, but it had very little substance. She started looking at her man beyond the worldly eye, the career, the clothes, the look, and found that he wasn't the kind of man that she wanted to raise a family with and live happily ever after. She discovered that he wasn't really into Tracee as much as he was into

Tracee's lifestyle. He got major points with his boys going to the Grammys and walking the red carpet.

When Tracee announced that she was considering leaving her job and taking the platinum parachute, he lost it.

"What the fuck is wrong with you?" he said. "You're such an ungrateful bitch! You have the best job in the world. People would kill to have your job, and you're just going to throw it all away. For what? For Jesus? Shiiiiit! That's the dumbest thing I ever heard."

Mr. Perfect had perfect grammar, but he also cursed like a ten-year-old in a schoolyard. Tracee was not going to be called a bitch by anyone, not even by Mr. Perfect in his Brooks Brothers suit. If he spoke to her like that now, what would he be saying to her in five years? Would he go from punishing her with his mouth to punishing her with his fist? Of course he would.

She decided it wasn't worth explaining—at least not to him. She was going to follow her heart, and that meant walking out on the "perfect" job and the "perfect" man in search of a *real* perfect life. She never looked back. But there were times when she felt incredibly lonely. There weren't many people from her old circle who understood what she was doing and why. Not even Ritz. Ritz tolerated Tracee's changes. She accepted them. But Ritz didn't understand them. There were many things Tracee could no longer talk to her friend about—like men.

Celibacy was not something Tracee ever set out to practice. She just said she wasn't having sex with anyone until the right one came along. The problem was that Mr. Right seemed to be taking his time. And as much studying and reading and going to church as Tracee was doing, she was still a human being with human needs. She wasn't like some women, praying for a man, begging God for Mr. Right. But she did indulge in fantasy every now and then. She would allow herself a taste of some eye candy and some mind candy. Tracee knew when she was close to improving herself, she would be in a position to receive that man. She was always of the mind that you would never find the right man until you were right within yourself. Somewhere, long ago and far away, she had read:

Marriage can make a good life great. Marriage cannot make a bad life good.

She had never forgotten that advice. In fact, she lived by it.

"Why in the world would God do that to some good man by having him get involved with a woman who wasn't right?" Tracee would say to the women in her church. "That is not love, that is biology, a natural reflex, like scratching an itch. Fix yourself first, be a good woman, and you will attract to you what you are. He will come to you."

Tracee wondered if her man had just come to her. She couldn't quite explain it, but it seemed as if she knew this Randolph Jordan. She felt like she knew him well.

And as Tracee daydreamed, Cecil and Madalyn were having a similar experience about Randolph.

"Cecil, did that young man seem familiar to you?" Madalyn said. She was frowning.

"He seemed very nice, but I don't know about familiar."

"He looked very familiar to me. You know I don't forget a face."

"Baby, I know that for a fact," Cecil said. "You think you've seen him somewhere before?"

"Yes, I think he is someone I've seen before," she said. "Or someone very much like him."

"Who?" asked Cecil.

"He called himself Randolph, but he reminds me of someone named Ritchie."

"'Richie'? Like Richie Rich, the cartoon character?"

"No, Ritchie with a *t*. Like 'Ritgina.'"

"Like who?"

"Like Ritchie Jordan. Ritz's daddy."

Ruff decided to throw a WHOT Block Party/Welcome Back Ritz Party in Washington Square Park in the West Village of Manhattan. He pulled some strings to get a park permit. He contacted the head of publicity at Universal Music Group and booked a couple of the hottest artists to perform. Station manager Abigail Gogel was not in agreement with any of it.

"So not only are we not firing that Ritz Harper, but we're throwing her a fucking party?!" she said. "I don't know who is crazier—you for coming up with the idea, or me for going along with it. I don't know, Ruff. I don't know about this."

"We will get mucho media attention. And we can make some money through sponsorship packages," said Ruff. "Besides, Ritz wants to come back big. She wants a spectacle. She said she wants to show people that she's not scared.

What better way than a big, splashy, public event? You got to give it to her. She has balls."

"Yeah. She's got balls, all right. Maybe she can do us all a favor and get shot again!"

"Come on, Miss Gogel!"

"You want publicity?! Now, *that* would bring us a lot of attention. In fact, it would be nice if Ritz could get her ass shot every four months or so, when they issue the new Arbitron book. I'll speak to her about it. I'll tell her she should be a 'team player.'"

"I don't want it like that," said Ruff, trying not to laugh. "I know how you feel about Ritz. But she has been a cash cow for us. How many people would come back from being shot and fight so hard to get back on the air? I respect that lady. I respect her a lot."

"Only because I respect you, I'll keep my thoughts to myself from now on," she said. "But I still wouldn't mind seeing her fat behind get drilled again. Okay, let's change the subject."

"Okay. How's your love life?" Ruff sneaked out a chuckle.

"That's enough, smart-ass."

Even though Ritz was weeks away from being back on the air, the party would be a way for her fans to celebrate her recovery and that she was alive. Ruff thought it would be a great idea, and he rounded up Ritz's team to help. Jamie, Aaron, and Chas were called to the office and told the news. They all agreed to do anything that needed to be done. Ruff wanted them to man a Ritz Harper booth where they would sell Ritz Harper T-shirts, hats, and mugs, and give away auto-graphed promotional pictures.

"But Ritz won't be there," Chas said.

"I know, but her team will be. Trust me, people will be happy to get a piece of her. She will be like the Wizard of Oz, there but not there. It'll work."

Ruff asked Chas to stick around after Aaron was sent back to man the boards. This was the first day of fill-in hosts, and he had to make sure everything was right.

Jamie had a lot of preparation to do for this woman Michelle Davis. Jamie didn't know what to expect from her, but she had made it known that she wanted to be tight, as she always was. She was excited. She had hopes of them taking their little thing to another level.

"Chas, I want to thank you for being a trooper," Ruff said. "Thank you for pitching in and making this hectic time less hectic. You are a real pro. I know it's been difficult. I know you had other plans, but you put all of that aside, rolled up your sleeves, and made it happen here. Thank you."

"I just want to win," Chas said. "I want to be number one."

"Do you think you can be number one with anyone who sits in that seat?" Ruff asked.

"I don't think I can. I *know* I can."

"Would it matter to you if Ritz didn't come back?" Ruff asked.

Is this a trick question? Chas thought. He had better be careful in answering this one.

Maybe Ruff was setting him up, trying to see where he

stood. He had to stay inside if he was ever to get what he really wanted. Chas was a patient man. What he wanted now more than anything was Ritz out of the way. But he couldn't have his fingerprints on that. Law No. 26 in the 48 Laws of Power states: Keep Your Hands Clean. "Maintain a spotless appearance by using others as scapegoats to disguise your involvement."

"Ritz is the diva. She is a fierce competitor and she loves to win," said Chas, not answering Ruff's question.

Ruff didn't pursue it. He thanked Chas again and told him that if he needed anything, to feel free to come to him.

☆ ★ ☆

Back in the studio, Aaron was feeling a little out of the loop and depressed.

"I miss Ritz," he confided in Jamie.

"Believe it or not, I do, too," Jamie said. "She was so crazy that she made the job interesting."

"I know. It was like we were creating something special here. We were being noticed. Even some of my friends were giving me props. Ritz talked to me so much on the air and let me go buckwild with the sound effects, it's like I had my own show within a show."

"I know. But I don't miss being the gofer. She was a bit much with that, and putting me on blast on the radio wasn't cool," Jamie said.

"She didn't do that to you often. You should have seen the last three interns. All she had them do was buy her super-size Kotex. She must have a goddamn Grand Canyon between her legs! They really got the hammer, and none of them lasted long. Ritz needed you. And even if she didn't say it, she appreciated you. I hope she comes back soon."

"Yeah."

"So who is this Michelle Davis bitch who is filling in for the week?"

"Watch that 'bitch' shit," Jamie shot back. "And boy, you need to up your game a bit. You don't know Michelle Davis? She's only the hottest up-and-comer in the news business. Fox News has her as their next big thing. I think she's very good. I don't know how she'll roll with radio, though."

"I hope she falls flat on her face!"

"Aaron! Come on, now. You have to be professional," Jamie warned.

"Don't worry, I'll be very professional. But she ain't getting none of my extras. No sound effects, none of the cute things that I do to make Ritz look good. If this Michelle Davis is so good, she's going to have to show it."

Chas walked back into the studio.

"Okay, team, you guys ready for today?" he said.

"Yes, sir. Ready and professional as can be," Aaron said, winking at Jamie. "So what did old Ruff want with you?"

"Nothing, just tying up some loose ends. Some programming stuff. So we have two guests booked for Ritz's fill-in. We might not get any callers, and I don't know if this lady knows how to work the audience. She's never done radio, so Aaron, I need you to be on point. I will be here to direct traffic for her, but if it blows up, we need to have a Ritz interview in the can ready to go. How about the interview when Ritz gets Heather Jones to admit she has herpes? We haven't used that in any of the *Best ofs*, have we?"

"No, we didn't use that one," Jamie jumped in. "And how about the interview with the pedophile who called up? I didn't use that one either. Ritz is up for an Edward R. Murrow Award for that."

"That's great. Cool. Well, we're ready."

"When is Ritz coming back?" Aaron asked.

"You miss her, huh, li'l fella?" Chas said teasingly. "I don't know. But I do know it will be soon. Miss Thing is about to bust at the seams, and I know they're about ready to kick her out of the hospital. Can you imagine her coming back from being shot and in a coma and being more fierce than ever? Ritz Harper is hell on wheels."

"That's what I'm talking about," Aaron said. "That's what I miss. That *fi-ya!*"

Jamie didn't say a word.

"What's going on with you, baby girl?" Chas asked Jamie.

"Nothing. Nothing at all."

"How are you and that fine hunk of a man doing?"

"Oh, he'll be here right after the show to pick me up," Jamie said. "We're doing well."

"You are so lucky that he's completely straight, or I would

be trying," said Chas, who wasn't "visibly" gay but certainly wasn't in the closet. "I ain't going to lie. I can see what he's packing under those clothes."

"You can't even imagine," Jamie said, pushing Chas playfully. "As a matter of fact, scratch that. I don't want you imagining. Take your dirty mind off my man."

"No need to worry. I'm not the kind of man who likes to chase after a man who I know is straight. I don't need the ego boost if I can get him over to my side. That's a waste of time. And I don't have any to waste. Besides, there are plenty of sexy available men out there who want to be had."

It was one thing for Chas to talk about Derek to Jamie. She didn't mind that at all. It was harmless. Jamie was used to women flirting with Derek. He had something about him that was so damn attractive. Jamie wasn't the jealous type. She never let a man get that close that he could make her jealous. She would just as soon walk away from a relationship than be played out. Derek made it easy being with him. He never even looked at another woman. He made her feel perfectly secure. He wasn't a dog. She knew he wasn't an angel, either. But at least he was real genuine and honest.

The only time she felt remotely uncomfortable was the last time Derek came up to the studio, when Ritz was overtly flirtatious with him. It wasn't Ritz's action, it was Derek's reaction to it. Ritz came over to him during the break and leaned across him to get a pen on the other side of his seat.

"Excuse me," Ritz purred.

Derek didn't say a word. He nodded, and it looked like for a split second Ritz and Derek's eyes locked and Derek blushed. In all the time Jamie had known Derek, she had never seen him blush; she didn't think he was capable of it.

What the fuck is that nigga blushing about? Jamie thought.

When they hooked up later that evening, she would find out.

18

"Welcome to the Ritz Harper Excursion. I am your hostess for the week, Michelle Davis. You may have seen me on Fox News, but now I'm on the radio, filling in for my girl, Ritz Harper. We hope she gets well and back on the air real soon. We're going to do something called Open Mic Monday, where you guys can call up and talk about anything on your mind. We can talk about the war in Iraq, this gully president of ours, the economy, and oh yeah, we can talk about some celebrities. I know quite a few, so we can dish the dirt if you want to. The number to call is 1-888-555-RITZ."

Michelle Davis felt very comfortable, more comfortable than she thought she would. Radio was different from television. Television was so scripted. The producers told you what to say, how to say it, where to stand. There was hair, makeup, and clothing concerns. Everything was about projecting a certain image of authority and perfection. Fox was one of the best at image shaping. They had created a star in Sean Hannity, a limited personality with an even more limited intellect. But they paid a superior person to sit with him each night and make him look good and give him credibility, and it had paid off. Hannity was a cash cow for the network.

Bill O'Reilly, another talking head who had severe limitations, was given a format that was perfect for his brash, no-nonsense style. He came off like a news version of John Wayne. People loved him. They were grooming Michelle to be a combination Oprah/Christiane Amanpour—serious journalist with a real-people feel.

Radio had never been on Michelle's radar. She was a rising star in a much bigger game. The starting salary in radio in a major market might be six figures, depending on the size of the station. In television, you could easily be looking at seven figures. Radio personality Glenn Beck jumped to television back in 2006 and saw a big seven-figure contract that called for hiring a couple of his radio producers, too. All of this for a one-hour show on an offshoot station. It wasn't even CNN, but their stepchild, Headline News.

Michelle Davis had the buzz. She was the next "It" girl. And now she was filling in for the most talked-about radio personality in the world—Ritz Harper. She was going to make the most of the opportunity. At the very least, she wasn't going to embarrass herself. And she was determined to have some fun.

"Okay, let's go to our first caller. Mike, you're calling from Detroit on our affiliate WCHB. What's on your mind today?"

"Hey, sexy. I love watching you on Fox, you fox!"

"Why, thank you, fine sir. But I know you didn't call just to say that."

"No, you're right, but I had to get that out. So do you believe that Ritz got what was coming to her?"

"Ooooh. Well, what do you mean?"

"Do you think she had it coming? For all the reckless stuff she does on the air, do you believe that her shooting was just a matter of time?"

Michelle squirmed in her seat just a bit.

"Now, I don't believe that anyone has something like that coming," she said. "My daddy taught me that people fight and hit and stuff when they can't think. So whoever shot Ritz is just dumb. But there is a larger issue to be discussed, and something I'm going to toss back to you, the audience—and thank you for your call, Mike [that was the cue for Aaron to hang up on the caller]—do you guys think we need to talk about people, put their business on Front Street? Do you guys really care about Britney Spears—is that front-page news? Or Christie Brinkley's husband? And why do we care about who's screwing whom? To tell you the truth, sometimes I just don't want to hear it.

"I mean, look at Whitney Houston and Bobby Brown. I read in the *Daily News* that they split up because Bobby has taken up with the Video Vixen, Karrine Steffans, also known as 'Superhead.'

"All I can say is, Whitney, honey, you have pipes that are a gift from God. I know you will be back. And please don't take that sorry-ass husband of yours back. Let the cut be clean and permanent. That's *your* prerogative, baby! We love you!"

The phone lines lit up. Ruff was listening from the office, and he liked what he heard. It was different—*very* different—from what the listeners of WHOT were used to hearing.

Michelle Davis. Ruff thought that she was just another blown-dry blowhard from TV Land. But that little riff she just did was very clever. Ruff listened.

Michelle continued:

"Tonight, I don't just want to talk about celebrity gossip crap and what famous star is sticking what body part in what orifice of some other famous star. Who cares?

"I want to talk about how you can get rich. I want to talk about owning homes and having power. Any of you folks ever hear of a man named Tony Brown? Probably not, but I'll tell you about him.

"Tony Brown said that the only color that *really* matters in this country is not black, it is not white. It is *green*—the color of money. Think about that. Yeah, we all have to love our fellow man, and do good works, and help the poor, and all the rest.

"But we also have to know where our next meal is coming from. We also have to know that we can cover the rent this month. If you can't do that, then you can't do anything. You gotta learn to walk before you can run.

"Ya'll saw Katrina. I'm trying to make sure that something

like that never happens to me or mine. I also want to talk about where to find some good men and some good friends, because it seems like we forgot how to do that.

"I want to talk about respecting our elders. When did it become okay to cuss an elder out? But I hear it all the time in the streets. And when did it become okay for folks to be calling each other nigga in the streets? Didn't people die so we wouldn't have to be called that? Now we're throwing it around like we're saying, 'What's up, brotha?' Come on, now, we can do better than that, can't we?"

Jamie was the call screener. Normally, she had to weed out the whack jobs who should get on the air from the whack jobs who shouldn't. Now she was actually getting some intelligent callers from all over the country who wanted to get in on the conversation. Jamie was actually having fun.

"Okay, we have Malachi from Milwaukee, it's Open Mic Monday on the Ritz Harper Excursion. I know it's a little different trip today, but what do you want to talk about?"

"First, sister, I want to thank you. I'm really feeling you. I just tuned in for the first time by accident and caught what you were saying, and I want you to know, you're right on! We have to start working on things that will build us up as a community. There is a lot going on in the world right now, and the last thing we need to focus on is what's happening with Lil' Kim, or some other rapper or actor. Who cares?!

"We're in World War Three. How am I going to keep my family safe? Have you seen the gas prices? How am I going to save money or make money in this environment? That's what we need to talk about!"

"Thank you, Malachi," said Michelle. "And I agree with you about World War Three. It may not be something folks want to talk about, but I agree. It is getting real hectic out there. And if and when one of those *allah akbar* types decides to really bring it over here—you think September 11 was something, imagine living in Beirut or Iraq or Afghanistan or Israel or Darfur, where stuff like that is happening every other day—will you still care if Trina and Missy Elliott are still an item, or Kimora Lee and Russell, or Jay-Z and Beyoncé? And what about Serena? Does it matter to you that she really wants to be an actress instead of the number-one female tennis player in the world, or whether she really prefers white men over black men? I say wish them all well. Let's move on!

"When that stuff hits the fan, they won't be targeting the president and his crew, and they damn sure won't send a memo out to black folks telling us to not go to a particular place on a particular day because they are going to bomb it. We are all in this together. It's time we wake up and get serious about our lives."

Michelle knew coming in that this fill-in spot was a risk for her. It wouldn't jeopardize her television career, but it wouldn't help it, either, if she bombed. She had decided that she wasn't going to do "Ritz Radio." She was going to do it the way she wanted to do it. She respected Ritz's hustle. She respected her climb to the top. But that wasn't Michelle's flow.

She looked at the phone lines and they were all lit up, like little stars in the sky. She smiled. It was working.

"Hello, Betty from the Bronx!" she said.

☆ ★ ☆

When Michelle had first met with Ruff, she told him that she wanted to do the show *her* way and he had said, "No problem." And she was doing it. She could tell, however, that Ritz's producer, Chas, wasn't too happy. He hadn't said two words to her. He had booked two guests for the show and was basically staying out of the way. Aaron, the engineer, seemed bored. There wasn't much chance for him to use his sound effects, which had made him so much a part of Ritz's show without even saying a word. But she could tell that Jamie was ecstatic.

"Do you need anything, Miss Davis?" Jamie asked during the break.

"No, thank you, sweetie. I didn't know what to expect, so I brought my own water." She took a swig from her Poland Spring sports bottle. She was so glad that she didn't have to worry about smudging her lipstick. It felt good to wear sweats, throw on a scarf, and still be at work. She got a tingle when she thought: *No one can see me.* Knowing that—being able to forget the makeup, and the hair, and the smile—set her free.

"Okay. I just want you to know that I think you're doing a wonderful job," Jamie said.

"You think?" Michelle asked. "That's really kind of you. I have to admit, I was really nervous. You know, Ritz has a certain kind of audience. And I didn't know how they would accept me."

"Well, look at the phone lines—they're all lit up," Jamie said. "And everyone wants to talk about what you're talking about."

The next three hours and forty-five minutes seemed to breeze by. People called in and wanted to talk about everything from Israel, to what to do about their retirement packages, to reality television. A few people did want to talk about Ritz Harper and how much they missed her, but they were quick to tell Michelle how much they were enjoying her, too.

She handled the guests with ease. The first was Thomas Lopez-Pierre, a guy who started a social society called The Harlem Club. Men had to pay a fee of twenty-five hundred dollars to join, and Lopez-Pierre claimed that all members were wealthy lawyers, investment bankers, and entrepreneurs.

Their goal was to meet and greet attractive women of a certain class. So the club had women submit photos—full-length, head-to-toe, preferably in swimsuits—and a bio. The women had to be single, under the age of forty, with a degree and no children. A committee screened the pictures, and if they were selected, the women didn't have to pay a fee to join.

The way Michelle Davis attacked Thomas Lopez-Pierre should be in a textbook about how to conduct an interview. She dissected him like a heart surgeon and did it all with a smile. By the end of the interview, she hadn't gotten Lopez-Pierre to cry uncle, but she had certainly exposed him. It was fun for Michelle and the audience. Even Lopez-Pierre enjoyed it, which seemed a bit odd to Michelle.

"You made me look so bad," he said as he was leaving. "I love that! Do you know that actually gets more women to join the club? I don't know what it is about you women, but the worse you're treated, the more you seem to love a man."

"I respect your honesty," Michelle said, chuckling with him. "And you know what—if a woman is dumb enough to fall for your crap, she deserves it. But please leave now. You are making me slightly nauseous."

Aaron escorted Thomas out. Michelle and Jamie just looked at each other and started cracking up.

"Do you think he's for real?" Jamie asked.

"Hell no," Michelle said. "He's completely full of shit. But I like him. Because he knows he's full of shit. He's just seeing how much of the shit he can get away with. Apparently, it's a lot. And it doesn't hurt that he's *foine*."

"Oh, you noticed? You were so busy busting his ass on the air, I didn't think you noticed."

"A sister ain't blind," Michelle said. "I noticed. I ain't blind and I ain't dumb, either. There ain't enough fine in the world to overlook that kind of behavior. Hell no!"

"I heard that!" cried Jamie. She gave Michelle a high five.

Michelle was feeling really good about the experience. In television there was so much backstabbing and backbiting that you could never let down your guard. You had to always be professional and never really be yourself. Someone was always watching, critiquing, and looking to throw darts. You had to have on heavy armor and be in defense mode at all times. It felt good for Michelle to be able to let her hair down and be real.

Little did she know that she needed heavy armor here, too—perhaps heavier than she could imagine.

19

Madalyn and Cecil had gone to the cafeteria to get something to eat. Tracee was in the waiting area outside of Ritz's room, reading. Tracee was at Ritz's beck and call, but Ritz hadn't beckoned so far. The nurses were on their toes, but Ritz would rather have Tracee help her to the bathroom, help her eat, and other personal stuff like that.

Tracee had her head buried in a book when the door opened.

It was Randolph. He had taken a break from his duties and decided to see if Ritz was up for a visitor.

"Hi . . ."

"I'm Tracee. I don't think I told you that yesterday."

"No, I'm sorry for being rude and not asking. I was a little nervous," Randolph said. "I only met Miss Harper once and I felt like I might be overstepping my bounds by coming by.

But when I heard she was shot and then found out she was on the very floor I was working on, I wanted to stop by and let her know that I was praying for her."

"I'm sure she will love to hear that," Tracee said. "Let me go in and see if she's up."

Tracee cracked the door to see that Ritz was indeed up, and she was watching CNN's *Morning Show*.

"Hey, Ritzy. You have a visitor."

Ritz's smile turned into a grimace.

"I don't want to fucking see anybody! Do you see what I look like?" snarled Ritz. She had finally looked in the mirror. While the swelling had gone down considerably and the bruises around her eye were fading, she still was a long way away from the fabulous "Ritz Harper."

"Who is it?"

"Randolph? He said he fixed your Jacuzzi."

"Tall, chocolate, Morris Chestnut–looking brother?"

"Yeah," Tracee said. "That's him."

"Oh, fuck no! He's the *last* person I want to see in this condition. That reminds me—I need to get some makeup and a wig, pronto. If motherfuckers are going to just be dropping by, I need to have some sort of defense. Tell him I'm not up to seeing anyone just yet. Tell him he can come by in a couple of days."

"Okay. Hey, were you and this guy trying to start something?"

"I was, for sure," Ritz said, and broke into a smile. "But he said something about saving himself for marriage or some shit. But I know I can break his ass down. You know how I do. Just give me a couple of weeks of rehab and I'll be back to my old self. I can't wait."

Shoot! Off-limits! Tracee thought. But it didn't matter. Tracee wasn't running after any man. If he or anybody wanted her, they would have to do the pursuing. And if Ritz wanted him, Tracee couldn't.

"Are you sure you don't want to see him? He doesn't seem like the type to care about how you look."

"I don't give a fuck what he cares about," Ritz shot back. "*I* care about how I look. Look at my hair, for crying out loud! Where is my fucking wig? Where is my pocketbook? Where is my left tit? I swear, I am gonna fucking *sue* some-body!!"

"Okay. Okay," Tracee said, and walked out. Randolph was sitting, thumbing through one of Tracee's books. It was Joel Osteen's *Your Best Life Now.*

"This is a great book," Randolph said. "I watch him every chance I get. But how does he know how to wrap up his ser-mon at *exactly* nine twenty-seven A.M., so they have three minutes left for commercials? He must have a gift!"

"Yeah, I'm almost finished with his book. I am really en-joying him. I haven't watched him much on television. I don't watch much TV."

"Me either, but when I do, it's Joel, Creflo, a few others. Do you go to church?"

"I actually live in Florida. I was only in town to hang out with Ritz for her big Grammy debut," Tracee said. "Since I've been here, I've gone to Faith Temple. I went on Sunday. I may go back this Sunday. Pastor Lakes is very on point."

"Isn't he that minister who was involved in a gay relationship or something?" Randolph asked.

"Yep. That's him. I'm not going to sit here and defend him. I'll just say that the sermon he preached on Sunday eliminated all doubt from my mind that he is truly a man of God. That's all I need to know. I don't know a single person who hasn't done something they wish they hadn't or made a mistake in their life. I know I made my fair share and probably will make many more before my life is over. They say you know a tree by the fruit that it bears. Pastor Lakes's fruit is plentiful."

"If you don't mind and if you are definitely going, I'd like to go to church with you one Sunday," Randolph said. He took a business card out his pocket. "The number on the bottom is my cell. Call me if you're going."

Randolph had become so engrossed with Tracee, he almost forgot why he was there.

"Oh, how's Ritz? Is she up to some company?"

"Uh, not really," Tracee said. "She's still a little out of it. Maybe you can come back in a couple of days."

"Do you mind if I come back tomorrow?"

"Um, uh, Ritz won't be ready to see anyone for a couple of days."

"Can I come back tomorrow to see you?" Randolph said.

Tracee felt a warmth flush from the back of her neck to her cheeks. She didn't know what to say. Of course, she wanted to see him tomorrow, and the next day, and the next day. But Ritz wanted him. She had to stand down.

"Uh, you can come back in a couple of days when Ritz is feeling better," Tracee said.

Randolph was a bit stung, but he got the message. The answer was no.

"Okay. But I still want to go to church if you're going. That's all about Jesus. You wouldn't want to keep me away from the Lord, now would you?" He feigned a pout.

Tracee laughed.

"If I go, I'll definitely call you." She could really dig this guy. A lot.

20

The day had taken its toll on Delilah. She got up at five in the morning after an evening of tossing and turning. She didn't really sleep well the night before. A lot was riding on this. It might be her last chance to get back to the top perch she once held. It might be her last chance for a comeback.

There was the hour and a half in makeup and hair. The microdermabrasion treatments, Botox, and electrolysis took care of the blotches, the wrinkled forehead, the lines around her mouth and eyes, and the unwanted hair above her lip and under her chin. She had really let herself go.

But she knew she had to snap back quickly. Delilah had three weeks from the day her agent told her about the screen tests at CNN to shed fifteen pounds and get back into the shape she was in before Ritz Harper had taken her out, where she had been reduced to spending days on end in bed—eating microwave pizza, Dove bars, peanut butter right out of the jar (without a spoon)—and plotting revenge.

She did a week of absolutely no carbs. That was good for knocking off five pounds. It made her bitchy as hell, but it didn't matter. Delilah didn't have any real friends to be bitchy around, and her agent, business manager, and accountant were used to her ways. They could tolerate her. It was business for them.

The second week, Delilah took it up a notch and did the Master Cleanse—a fast of lemon juice, distilled water, and maple syrup with cayenne tincture. She learned about this fast one day while watching one of the talk shows. Actor Danny Glover, "Mister" from *The Color Purple*, was talking about his campaign against cabdrivers in New York City who would not pick up blacks. It happened to him, and he was determined to let the world know that racism still existed in America. But what interested Delilah was how great he looked. Danny Glover was pushing sixty, but he had the body of a thirty-year-old.

"And he hasn't had any work done," Delilah muttered to herself. "He looks fabulous."

Delilah, a television junkie who studied everybody on the screen, could tell what kind of plastic surgery or other procedures a person had done by just looking at them. She even knew how long ago they had it and when they would need something again. The interviewer asked Glover about his great physique and he mentioned some fast he was on. He was doing it for forty days, and he said it gave him so much energy that he never felt better.

"He's crazy with that forty days of no eating stuff," said Delilah, who had grown comfortable talking to the television. "But it sounds interesting."

She went online and looked it up.

What the hell, she thought. *If it kills me, it can't be worse than the life I'm living now.*

Delilah never knew how dependent she had grown on being a star. It wasn't her career, it was her *life*. She was *The* Delilah Summers, the best in her business, the go-to person for any major interview with any major public figure. Delilah loved everything that went with being Delilah Summers. She liked the chauffeur-driven cars, the star treatment at every fancy restaurant in Manhattan. She never needed a reservation, and at certain spots, she even had a special table no matter when she came in. She was Delilah Summers. People wanted her autograph. Clerks at department stores fawned all over her on the occasions she went to Saks or Bloomingdale's to shop. She had her own special room and her own special shopper, who brought her any item she desired.

She got free champagne and finger sandwiches when she shopped. She got the star treatment because she was a star. She got to walk around with her head in the air, because she was Delilah Summers.

Her fall was hard. It wasn't long before all the star trappings disappeared. Now, if she wanted a stupid finger sandwich, it would be for cash only, up front. Even the way people looked at her changed. That was the hardest part, realizing that all of the attention was phony. People only liked her because she was a "star." They didn't like *her* for who she was. The realization that she didn't really have friends, just sycophants and yes-people, was hard to take. For most of her life, Delilah Summers was surrounded by people—whether they were men who wanted to sleep with her, or girlfriends who wanted to be like her, or agents who wanted to make money off of her, or moochers who wanted to sponge off her. Now she was really alone. Even her agent was there only because he knew she could make a comeback, and that would be fifteen percent of a seven-figure deal in his pocket.

She was going to be different this time around. Delilah was going to be more sincere, less self-absorbed, less caught up in herself, more willing to do the small things. She did the screen test, even though she was insulted by it. She got over that and knocked them dead.

The crash diet made her suits fit perfectly. She looked fantastic. She never lost her talent to deliver the news with punch and verve. She even displayed something she never did before—a self-deprecating humor.

"Hell, if I can't laugh at myself after what I just went through, I might as well hang it up," she said to the producer of her screen test after she nearly fell out of a broken seat right in the middle of her delivery. The old Delilah would have demanded someone's head on a platter after such a "humiliation." The new Delilah simply said, "Now, if I had fallen on my behind on the air, that would have been great television!" And she kept it moving.

Delilah wasn't surprised when the call came in at 1:35 in the afternoon. She was flipping the channels between Charlie Rose on PBS, CNN, and Jerry Springer. She loved Jerry and Maury and the judge shows. They helped her feel better about herself. Seeing all of those dysfunctional people let Delilah know that her little scandal wasn't that big of a deal. That she could definitely rise above it all. She was a daytime show junkie. She even grew to appreciate the magic of Oprah. Before her fall, Delilah was a big-time Oprah Hater. She couldn't understand how that "fat, phony bitch" had become such a huge star.

"Huge star" was kind of an understatement. *She was the richest woman in the goddamned world.* And the money was hers, all hers—not like other "richest women," like the Queen of England. Queen Elizabeth couldn't just buy the Crown Jewels and give them to Prince Philip as a Christmas present. Her fortune was in name only.

But Oprah could buy the Crown Jewels if she so chose, then give them to Stedman as a stocking stuffer!

I have more talent in my upper lip than she does in her whole big body, Delilah used to think.

But sitting home, watching Oprah—more to criticize, at first, than to actually *see*—she began to understand why Oprah was *Oprah*. Oprah really *did* want to make a difference on this earth. Oprah wasn't fake, and people knew that instinctively. Oprah, had she not been *real*, would have been gone and forgotten twenty years ago, like Morton Downey, Jr., and the hundreds of others who had tried and failed at the talk-show game.

Delilah wanted to be like Oprah, too. Could she be?

Shoot. Why *couldn't* she be? What did she have left to lose? She had already lost everything!

Since the screen test, she didn't do much TV watching. She started going to the gym, started reading more, surfed the Internet, and started keeping a journal.

And remarkably, as time passed, she spent less and less time thinking about Ritz Harper. Before, she'd been fueled by revenge. There wasn't a happier person in the world than Delilah Summers the night Ritz Harper was shot. And when she found out that Ritz had lived, she seethed, trying to figure out how she could get someone to kill her for real the next time. She wanted to see Ritz dead, or in ruins, or preferably both.

The diet and the exercise were starting to show their effects. She was feeling so much better, both in body and in mind. She was healing. She was becoming a new person, a better person. Did she have Ritz Harper to thank for that?

Now, when she thought about Ritz Harper, the rage wasn't as hot as it had been. The rage used to be white-hot. Now it was down to red-hot.

Now, when she thought about Ritz Harper, she always remembered a proverb she had to memorize when she was in grammar school, a proverb she hated because she didn't know what it meant: *To understand all is to forgive all.*

Delilah still didn't get that. No. There are certain things that can *never* be forgiven, like having your life ruined for some Arbitron ratings.

But still, it was food for thought. . . .

When the phone rang just before 1:30 P.M. it was her agent, telling her that not only did CNN love the screen test but they were also prepared to give her a show starting in the fall, and that they were thinking about her as a replacement for Larry King, in case he ran off and got married again. Or maybe permanently, because next to Barbara Walters he was the oldest person on television.

"Delilah, you're back!" Frank Baker said. "I would suggest signing a one-year deal, because in one year you'll be back on the network scene and, I predict, even bigger than you were."

Delilah had a lot to prove to the public, and even more to prove to herself. Would it be better the second time around? Would it be different? Could she be as successful? Did it matter?

Delilah had so many questions, but only one answer: "I have nothing to lose!"

21

Randolph got the hint—Tracee didn't want him coming by every day, but he wanted to. He felt that she didn't really mean it, but he would honor her wishes. He couldn't stop thinking about her—her warm, girlish smile, those eyes, so big and bright that he swore he could literally see right into her soul. He smiled. She had him.

Pull the strings, and I'll sing you a song,
I'm your puppet . . .
Make me do right, or make me do wrong,

Some folks found the Word in the Bible. Randolph found his word in 1960s R&B. All the answers were there.

Of course, Tracee had a beautiful face—without makeup, no less. And yes, she had what looked like a banging body.

But there was a purity about Tracee that he hadn't seen in a woman in a long, long time, not since the woman whose name he still couldn't say. Tracee didn't have any pretenses or hang-ups. She had a confidence that didn't need to be advertised. It was just there.

Some women wear their confidence like a slinky red dress. They want you to know that they're something. Tracee just *was*. Randolph knew that there was so much more to her, and he wanted to know it all. When he checked into the hospital every morning and got his men working on whatever project they were going to tackle for the day, he would walk by Ritz's room, thinking, hoping that he would bump into Tracee outside.

But on this morning, Randolph ran into Maddie and Cecil on the floor. Cecil had his arm around Maddie. They looked so bonded, so together, so *as one*. Randolph could feel it. Here were these two old folks, but they emitted a *power*— a power that was as strong, and eternal, as sunlight.

"Good morning!" Randolph said.

"Hello, son," Cecil said. Cecil called every man under the age of fifty "son."

"What are you two up to?"

"We're just about to go out and get some air. Sitting around a hospital all day can make you sick," said Maddie, who did look pale and sick. "Um, you're a friend of Ritz's? What did you say your name was again?"

"Randolph. Randolph Jordan."

"Jordan?" Maddie said.

"Um, yes, ma'am," said Randolph, shifting from one foot to another. He didn't like the tone of Maddie's voice, and he suddenly realized that he was afraid of her. This was not a woman whom he could dazzle with his smile, and his good looks, and his glib tongue. This was not a person whom he could fool, like he had fooled so many women earlier in his life. He was looking at power—*real* power. He couldn't believe it, but his knees started to tremble.

"Where are you from, Randolph?"

"I was born in Richmond, Virginia, ma'am. But my parents moved up north when I was two."

Maddie looked at Cecil.

"Cecil, doesn't this boy remind you of somebody? Forget the rest of him and look at his eyes. You can always tell by the eyes."

Cecil squinted his old eyes and looked hard at the young, deep-mocha-complexioned man who stood in front of him, six feet two inches tall, with broad shoulders and a barrel chest, perfect teeth and bulging muscles.

Then he remembered what Maddie said and he looked into Randolph's eyes.

Yes. . . .

He knew those eyes. He had seen those eyes before. But where? Where?

Then, suddenly, he knew:

He saw those eyes years ago, at their house. Years ago, when Gina was there. Years ago, when he had called someone "Richie" and that person had said, "No, it's Ritchie, with a *t.*"

"Is your daddy Ritchie Jordan?" Uncle Cecil could barely get the words out.

"Yes," said a startled Randolph. "Do you *know* him?"

"Oh my, oh my," Maddie said.

Randolph could barely speak. "Please," he said. "What do you mean?"

Uncle Cecil put his hand on Randolph's arm, and Randolph felt like he had been touched by an electric current. This man, like his wife, had *power*—true power, the power that is never seen unless it chooses to be seen.

"If your father is Ritchie Jordan," Uncle Cecil said, "you are Ritz's brother."

22

When Jamie first came aboard the Ritz Harper Excursion, she was a bright-eyed, excited student, eager to learn everything she could from a woman who was what Jamie thought she wanted to become. There weren't many women in the radio game, and there weren't any women commanding the kind of attention and money that Ritz Harper was. Jamie figured she could learn at Ritz's knee, go to a smaller market, get some experience there, then come back to New York and take out a washed-up, semi-senile Ritz.

In this culture, a woman was considered to be a "hot babe" between the ages of eighteen and thirty-five, tops. But Jamie was realizing that didn't apply to women of color. Black don't crack. J-Lo, who was pushing forty, was still being written about in the tabloids as "bootylicious." Janet Jackson, who was in her early forties, was still getting her rhythm nation on, appearing on magazine covers with her eight-pack showing. Halle Berry, fortysomething. Nothing more need be said. Madonna, who was Italian (and you know what they say about Sicilians), was still holding it down, pushing fifty.

Jamie knew that while she didn't have much time to make her mark, she had more than enough time.

She had her plans all mapped out. She knew she was smarter than Ritz. But brains never mattered. The most successful were rarely the most intelligent. Intelligence is one of the least important traits to success. Guile, craftiness, having the right connections, and being cutthroat were way more valuable tools for success than intelligence.

Jamie watched her dad work his game in the corporate world. And while he made enough money to keep his family in a nice-sized home, in a beautiful, well-manicured neighborhood, and was able to send all of his children to college, he was not wealthy.

He was not the kind of wealthy that Jamie wanted him to be. On some level, her father was living a lie. He had to tuck his penis down and stick it between his butt cheeks, like a transvestite, and smile as he did it. He had to keep his mask on tight. By the time he came home, he was worn out. His job wasn't fun. Jamie never heard her father say that he liked what he did.

What's the point in going to school and working hard to spend twenty to thirty years doing something you absolutely hate? Jamie often thought.

The world of radio and entertainment was stressful, but the games and the characters, the wealth and excitement, and the unpredictability made it fun. Just thinking about it would get Jamie's adrenaline flowing.

But she was about to blow it all because she couldn't keep up the facade of being a good team player on the Ritz Harper Excursion.

Ritz was hard to work for before the shooting. She barked orders, she undermined and belittled everyone in the studio, including Chas. But she seemed to be doing it by accident, like some little four-year-old who lets fly with whatever is on her mind.

Only those who truly knew her understood that Ritz was not the unfeeling, nasty, horrible bitch that many thought she was.

Ritgina Harper was just a grown-up, big-boobed, big-wigged little girl who said whatever came to her mind. She spoke before she thought.

That was okay with little girls, but little girls who blurted out whatever came into their little heads did not have an audience of millions, like Ritz did.

There was a different edge to Ritz now, a more purposeful edge. She was not just mean and bitchy. She now seemed like she was on the prowl, like she was determined to destroy everything in her path. She would not be denied. Ritz was preparing to come back the following week. The station was setting up a studio in her home. They asked Jamie to help make the transition smooth.

She talked to Ritz in the days before her "comeback broad-cast," and Ritz was bitchier than ever.

"I want you to make sure that I have everything in place. I want to be better than before I left, so I need you to cover every little fucking detail, you got it?!" Ritz was talking to Jamie as if she were the most incompetent intern Ritz had ever worked with, bar none. Ritz spoke to her like she was some dumb-ass, snot-nosed kid who didn't know what the hell she was doing. Jamie resented the tone.

Jamie resented Ritz.

"Oh, and Jamie? I'll set up a room for you in my house. I want you to be there twenty-four/seven to take care of anything that may come up. That won't be a problem, will it?"

"No, Ritz" is what Jamie's mouth said. *Oh hell no, who the fuck does she think she is?* was what her mind was saying. *That bitch wants me to be her nursemaid? I know she just got shot, but is she crazy, too?*

Jamie was on the brink of depression. Working with Ritz again was making her hate her job. She was starting to hate her life. The man whom she thought she could love had unceremoniously dumped her. The last time they met at the studio, he drove her home without saying much. He parked in front of her house and without looking at her said, "We need to cool it."

Jamie was expecting something totally different. She was looking forward to him saying they needed to take things up a notch, maybe even invite her to move in with him. That's how well she thought it was going. To hear him say "We need to cool it" was like a punch in the stomach. The air was knocked out of her, and it took Jamie a minute to actually digest what he said.

"Wha . . . what?" she whispered, trying to find her voice.

"Babe, we need to cool it," he said, still not looking at her.

"But why? What's going on?!"

"I have a lot going on right now, and I don't have the time, and it's not fair to you. We need to just cool it for a while."

"What if I don't want to cool it?" Jamie said.

"I'm sorry," said Derek, staring at the steering wheel. He refused to turn to look at her. He didn't want to look into those doelike eyes of hers and see any hurt. He didn't want to take that away as his last image.

Jamie had prided herself on not chasing after any man. She had never been broken down. She wouldn't give any man that satisfaction, but this time she was cut by Derek, cut deeply. So she decided to get out of the car before there was blood everywhere. She didn't look at Derek. Jamie just opened the door, got out, and slammed it shut.

So many questions were running through her head. She didn't understand what had happened or why. And the most frustrating part was that she didn't think her questions would ever be answered.

Derek sat for a minute outside of Jamie's home, collecting his thoughts. He did what he had to do. He didn't want her in the middle of what was going down. He also didn't want her in that way anymore. The last thing Derek wanted to do was to keep a chick around just because he could. He'd had "relationships" in the past where the woman knew what her purpose was, where she knew she was only there for physical play and nothing more. Jamie wanted more. Jamie needed more. Jamie deserved more. Derek thought he could give her more, but as soon as he realized that he couldn't, he had to let her go.

He wasn't one for many words. He wasn't going to break everything down for her. It was better for him if Jamie just hated him. It would make it easier for both of them.

As he drove away, he thought about the trip he would have to take in the morning to see his brother. He dreaded it. With Ritz Harper still alive, Derek knew Jayrod would be consumed with finishing the job. That conversation with Jayrod would be ten times more difficult than the one he had just had with Jamie. While she was in limbo and in a coma, it was easy to deal with Jayrod. But now that she was back—not just back but looking to regain her former perch on top—Jayrod was about to lose it. He wanted to get her more than anything. It was all he would talk about. It was all he thought about.

There was no way Derek could tell his brother how he really felt about Ritz Harper. How could he? He didn't even understand it himself. Derek had never been caught out there before—especially not behind a woman. But he was officially snagged. And it was with a woman he couldn't really have.

He could never be her man. At best, he could be her secret fuck buddy. But Derek feared he wanted more.

How ironic, he thought.

There was no way he could tell his brother that he thought he was in love with Ritz Harper. There was no way he could tell him that he just couldn't kill her.

23

"Maddie, sweetie, you have to get checked out," Cecil said. He looked worried. He'd been worried for a while. As much as Madalyn tried to hide how she was really feeling, she wasn't doing a good job. She looked pale and weak. And the recent coughing fits that kept her and Cecil up half the night sealed it.

"I know you don't like people telling you what to do, but we're taking you to a doctor the first thing in the morning," he said.

Madalyn didn't say a word. She knew she had to go. She also knew what they would say. She may have been able to hide many things from others, but she couldn't hide the truth from herself. Madalyn knew that as strong as she was and as strong as she wanted to be, she was sick, very sick.

The next day, the doctor confirmed what she knew.

"Mrs. Robinson, we have to do further tests, but it seems as if the cancer has spread," he said. "We are going to do everything we can. We may need to operate."

The color drained from Cecil's face. He had demanded to be in the examination room. He wanted to hear it for himself. He grabbed on to Madalyn, more to receive support than to give it. He had no clue what his life would be without her. He loved her more than he loved anything or anyone in his entire life. He loved his Maddie more than he loved himself. She gave him a will to live.

When he found out that she had cancer, Cecil went into nursemaid mode. He was the one to force her to make changes in her diet. He walked with her every evening after their light supper. He even tried to keep Madalyn laughing, which wasn't one of his talents. That made it all the more funny. Cecil had read somewhere that laughter accelerates healing, and he was willing to try anything. The side effects from the chemotherapy were tough to watch Madalyn go through. It wasn't just the vomiting, but she was rendered flat on her back most days. Madalyn was one of the most active people he knew. She was a bit of a busybody. She couldn't keep still. She had to be doing and going, in constant motion. To see her in the bed until noon and then drag around the house all day nearly broke his heart.

Then, right in the middle of this battle, they got the call that their little girl, Ritz, had been shot and she was fighting for *her* life. For a while, both Cecil and Madalyn forgot about the cancer. That was a mistake, because the cancer didn't forget about Madalyn.

"Doc, what are you saying?" Cecil said.

"We won't know for sure until we do further tests," the doctor said. "We'll run them as soon as possible. We'll have to admit Mrs. Robinson immediately. I would suggest you get your affairs in order."

Madalyn refused to cry. But Cecil's eyes were watering. He was fighting it, but he couldn't help it. He hadn't cried through the whole ordeal. Cecil excused himself. He went to the men's room and he broke down and sobbed. He had never cried like that in his entire life.

24

Ritz was healing well. The pain was subsiding and she was getting stronger every day. She knew she was feeling better when she started asking the doctor about when she could get her implant back instead of when she would be breathing normally again. The collapsed lung was better, as was her face, which was still tender in places but was beginning to look more like the old Ritz.

The staff at the hospital were growing tired of Ritz's diva-like antics. They were looking forward to the day when she got the hell out.

Dr. Grevious came in to tell her that she was less than two days away from going home.

"You're doing so well, Miss Harper, that we're going to spring you from this place," he said.

Ritz didn't wait for the doctor to give her the green light.

She had already made moves to go back on the air. She'd put the station and her team on notice. And she couldn't be happier. That meant she could get back to being the undisputed Queen of All Media. She could get back to her career.

"So what's the holdup, Doc?" she said.

"We want to make sure that no infection sets in. How's your breathing?"

"It's much better," Ritz said, taking a deep breath and pretending like it didn't hurt. "I'm doing a hundred percent better."

"I have some bad news, though," said the doctor, whose face turned serious.

"What's the matter?!" Ritz didn't really want to hear it. He had just said she could go home. What could be wrong?

"It's your aunt," he said.

"Aunt Madalyn? I know she's been here. I haven't had a chance to really talk to her."

"Well, she's been admitted to the hospital," he said. "I'll bring a wheelchair around to take you to see her."

"Admitted? What's the matter?!" Ritz said.

"I'm not at liberty to say," he said. "You should speak to her as soon as you can."

"Look, you need to tell me what's wrong with my aunt," Ritz could turn real nasty real quick. "What the fuck is up with this cryptic shit? Just tell me."

"I can't tell you, but she can if she wants you to know."

Ritz tried to get out of the bed.

"What room is she in?" she said.

"Miss Harper, please get back in bed," Dr. Grevious said. "The wheelchair will be here any minute. We don't need a relapse. You need your strength."

Ritz was tired of people telling her what to do. She wanted to get to her aunt and she was going, period.

Just as she was about to leave the room, a nurse came in with the wheelchair.

"Please take a seat, Miss Harper. Your aunt is one floor up. The nurse will accompany you," said Dr. Grevious.

Ritz took a seat and rode into the hallway. It was the first time she had been out of her room. It took a minute for Ritz to get used to the bright, hot fluorescent lights of the hospital hallway. She noticed for the first time the officer stationed outside the waiting area of her room. The officer followed her in the wheelchair discreetly.

Ritz hadn't thought of the potential danger she was in until now. And that was only a fleeting thought as she headed into the elevator to see her aunt. She thought about the things her mother had said to her, and how truly sorry she was to allow her ego to stop her from apologizing to her aunt. Aunt Maddie was right. Ritz had gone too far. She just didn't want to hear it. Whatever was wrong with Aunt Maddie, Ritz vowed to herself to be there for her.

Ritz was wheeled off the elevator, entourage in tow, and was led into a room two doors away from the elevator. It was a quiet floor; Ritz noticed that immediately. When she came, her aunt was sleeping. Uncle Cecil was in a chair next to the bed. He appeared to be nodding, too. The first thing Ritz noticed was that her aunt was bald. She hadn't put on her wig. She was too weak for vanity.

"Hey, Unc," Ritz whispered, not wanting to wake her aunt. "How's she doing?"

Uncle Cecil was a little startled. But he popped right up.

"She's resting, and that's good," he said. "The coughing fits keep her from sleeping. But the doctors gave her something that pretty much knocks her out."

"So what's the prognosis?"

Cecil hesitated. Should he tell her, or should Maddie tell her?

"It's not good, Ritzy," Cecil said. "I'm going to let your aunt tell you."

"Why won't anybody tell me *anything?*" Ritz whispered, but it was an angry, screaming whisper. "Uncle Cecil, please tell me what's the matter with Aunt Maddie! Please!"

Madalyn stirred from her sleep. She opened her eyes and saw Ritz at her bedside in a wheelchair.

"Hey, baby girl," Aunt Maddie croaked.

Cecil saw this as an opportunity to leave the two alone together.

"I'm going to the cafeteria to get a snack," he said, kissing Madalyn on the forehead and then bending over to kiss Ritz on the cheek. "I need some air. You two behave."

Madalyn smiled and Ritz playfully rolled her eyes.

"Auntie, what's up?" Ritz asked when they were alone. "What's going on?"

"I'm sick," Madalyn said.

"I can see that," Ritz said. "But before you tell me, I want to say something to you."

She got closer to the bed. She could smell the hospital smell, the disinfectant, the medicinal odors that somehow Ritz couldn't smell in her own room. She hated hospitals. She had avoided them her whole life. Now she was a patient *and* a visitor.

"I love you, Aunt Maddie. And I am sorry for hanging up on you and saying those mean things. I didn't mean it."

"Oh yes, you did," Maddie said, managing a smile.

"Okay, I did mean it. But I never meant to hurt you," Ritz said.

"Yes, you did, too."

"Okay, okay. You know me too well, don't you? But you know I never wanted us to go more than a year without talking. That was my fault. But you're pretty stubborn, too. You could have picked up the phone."

"I could have. And I probably should have, because I am more mature than you are."

Maddie smiled, then continued. "You'll be just as 'mature' when you're my age, child. I assumed you would call when you were ready to talk. I wasn't going to push you. You needed that time to feel your way."

Ritz stared at her.

"Yeah, I felt my way, all right. Right into a hospital room, shot full of holes. That's my excuse. Now, what brings *you* here?" she asked, reaching up and rubbing the smoothness of her aunt's head. "What happened to all of your beautiful hair?"

Maddie had had beautiful hair. It was her pride and joy. "Good hair," black folks liked to say about any hair that a comb could run through without getting stuck.

"I have cancer, Ritzy. They ran some tests yesterday and found that it has spread to my lymph nodes."

"What?!" Ritz screamed. "What does that mean? You're going to be all right, aren't you? There is something they can do, right? I've got the money, Auntie M. Do what you have to do. Buy whatever you need to get better! I'll pay! I'll pay cash!!"

"Ritzy, it doesn't look good, but I'm okay with it all. I didn't take care of myself the way I should have. I was stubborn. I guess that runs in the family. I thought my strength could just whip this thing. I was wrong."

Ritz winced. Did all of the worrying about Ritz contribute to her aunt's deterioration? Maddie looked terrible. Ritz needed to feel empowered, in control. She had money. She could make sure that her aunt got the best care money could buy. She would make it all better.

"Where is your doctor? I need to talk to someone about this!"

"My doctors in Virginia have been in constant contact with the doctors here," Madalyn said. "Everybody's doing the best they can."

"We're going to beat this, Auntie. I know we will. Look at me. I was supposed to be dead. Now they are talking about releasing me this week. When I get out, I'm going to throw a party or something, and I want you there."

"Forget all of the partying," Madalyn said. "Focus on a full recovery and don't worry about me. I'm in good hands. I have Cecil. The doctors have been wonderful. Tracee has been here for me."

"Tracee knows?!"

"She figured it out. And when I ended up here, it confirmed what she already thought. She's been great."

Ritz didn't say anything. She was jealous that her friend knew more than she did about her own family. Ritz was insanely jealous that Tracee in the last year had developed a better relationship with Ritz's aunt and uncle than Ritz herself.

"There is so much going on, so much to talk about," Madalyn said, then stopped. She wanted to tell Ritz about Randolph Jordan and her father, but one thing at a time.

Madalyn hoped there *would* be time.

25

Edwin was less nervous, less apprehensive than he had been last week. But the feeling of uncertainty still weighed in his soul. This Sunday would be the real litmus test of his forgiveness. The reporters and curiosity seekers would be gone, leaving Faith Baptist with its real congregation. There were already some who had walked out, saying they would never return. Deacon Templeton left for good, saying he couldn't be part of a church with a "fudge packer" for a pastor. He said he wasn't one of those "faggy Episcopals."

"Anyone who stays is going straight to hell with him," Deacon Templeton said before he stormed off.

Edwin understood the confusion. He just couldn't understand the anger and the venom. There were a few others who left, more out of embarrassment than hatred. Those folks had been coming to church for appearances. They loved being a

part of Faith Baptist when their pastor was featured in news-
paper articles and was on the cover of *Ebony*. They loved being part of something that everyone was talking about. They
tolerated Edwin's come-as-you-are policy, which let people
show up for church in jeans or a T-shirt. They even tolerated
his outreach to the prisons and the halfway house he built,
which brought "another element" into the church. But this
latest scandal was the last straw.

Their leaving was addition by subtraction, the way Edwin
saw it. He was glad to see them go. His philosophy was that
the only folks he wanted in his church were folks who wanted
to go to Heaven—and if he was left with only two congregants, he would build from there. That was God's will, as he
said last Sunday:

"The Lord Jesus left us with two commandments. Those
two commandments cover all of the rest. And they are to
love the Lord thy God with all thy heart, all thy soul, all thy
mind, and all thy strength. The second is to love one another
as Jesus has loved you. Now, with all you have heard this
morning and over the last few days, if you can't love me and
love this church, then you should not be here."

Edwin had purposely thrown down the gauntlet. What
was revealed about his previous life on Ritz Harper's radio
show was not just a test for Edwin. It was a test for his growing church and everyone in it. It was a test to see who was
really there for show and who was there "sho 'nuff" for God.

"This experience will separate the wheat from the chaff,"
Edwin said.

He prayed in his sanctuary as he did every Sunday. When he was done, he buttoned his shirt, tightened his tie. He left his robe hanging. He had decided the previous week that he was going to shake off the covering and come to the church without the pomp and circumstance, the royal garb, and all of that. He was but a sinner who wanted to become a saint.

But he was just like his flock, and he was going to show that a simple man can overcome anything and do the Lord's work.

Edwin walked out of the sanctuary and took his seat near the podium as the choir, the deacon, and the prayer leader performed their Sunday duties. He looked out at the crowd to survey what was left of his congregation. There were a few more empty seats than normal. His mother sat in the front row—her head held high, as always.

Mother Lakes, who had helped found the church with her husband, had been Edwin's rock. She and Edwin hadn't spoken much since "the event." But they didn't have to. Mother Lakes was a prayer warrior. She was a spirtual battler. She was vanquishing Edwin's enemies behind the scenes. And she was there for him. She was always there for him. Seeing his mother gave him comfort.

As Edwin scanned the other faces in the congregation, one was still absent—his wife, Patricia. He had called her every single day since Ivan Richardson had exposed him to the world. He called her every evening. She was staying with her mother and spending a lot of time at Kim's, too. Kim was one of the few women in the church to befriend Patricia, who was ostracized by the jealous single women because Edwin had chosen her to be his wife.

Patricia wouldn't speak to him, but she was big enough to let him speak to his kids. His boy only wanted to know, "Daddy, when are we coming home?"

"I don't know, son," Edwin said.

"Can you stay here with us, then?"

"No, son. But I love you. I'll see you soon. I promise." That was all Edwin could say.

It was a promise that wasn't up to him to keep. But he would keep it, indeed. His God would see to that. He understood Patricia's pain, her feelings of betrayal, but she couldn't keep him away from his babies.

Kim would take the phone and tell Edwin that Patricia wasn't ready to talk. Kim had been with her in the car, listening to the radio, when that man told the world everything about Edwin's secret past. They were having a "girls' day out," complete with spa treatment, lunch, and shopping. It was a rare time of fun for Patricia, who had a hard time making friends as the pastor's wife—especially when just about every single woman in the church had had their dibs on the very handsome, very elegant Edwin Lakes.

But Edwin chose Patricia, which made the women who wanted him—which was just about every one of them, single *and* married—green with envy. Patricia had poured her energies into being the perfect wife, the perfect church matron, the perfect mother. Kim befriended her and convinced her to start taking some time for herself. Ironically, on the day she finally did so—on her girls' day out—the whole day turned dark. Patricia felt more than betrayed. She felt like her entire life with Edwin had been a lie. She couldn't talk to him until that feeling subsided. She wondered if it ever would.

For Edwin, being without Patricia felt worse than being dead. She was his best friend, his confidante, the only person with whom he shared everything—well, *almost* everything. He was not just lonely, he was lost. The only place where he felt remotely like himself was in the pulpit.

He stood, ready to give his sermon.

He began his sermon with a parable about a fish:

"In nature there is a fish called the *Pardachirus marmoratus*," he started. "Don't worry, there will not be a test on this later. It took me two days to practice pronouncing it. It is called the Moses Sole—s-o-l-e—as in the sole fish, not your soul from heaven. It is a small fish found in the Red Sea, the same Red Sea that Moses parted when he led his people out of Egypt. Now, what's so special about this little fish? Well, it swims in some dangerous waters, among sharks, who would just love to gobble him up.

"Now, God is a genius. He created perfect balance and perfect harmony in his universe. He armed this fish, the Moses Sole, with protection. When in danger, the Moses Sole can secrete a milky, poisonous substance that can render a shark temporarily paralyzed. This tiny fish can take out a big, murderous shark.

"We, too, have been armed with a paralyzing poison—but it is poison only to those living outside of the will of God.

It's called God's Word. See, we have Jesus's Soul—s-o-u-l—inside of us. And we can render Satan and his minions paralyzed. We have been given the power of prayer, which can stop the devil in his tracks. We have been blessed with the truth, which will set us free.

"Now, last week, I stood in this pulpit and spoke the truth to you. I see there are quite a few who found that truth to taste like poison, and so they aren't here today. I'm sure that to them the poison from the truth tastes real nasty, too.

"I want to thank those of you who stood by me during these rough times. I love those who are not with us. But I really admire the strength and the courage of those who *are* here, to build this church and grow God's kingdom. I love you. Let's stay prayed up, let's stay in the Word, and let's keep in touch with Jesus' soul that is within all of us. We have to swim together and protect each other. Never forget: The sharks are always hungry. The sharks are never satisfied."

Then Edwin made a call for the altar. He asked anyone who was struggling with a problem, or who needed comfort, or who had a heavy heart, to come to the altar for prayer.

Tracee Remington got up. She needed to pray for Aunt Maddie, for her health and for God's will to be done. She also prayed for Ritz. She wanted to pray for Ritz's spiritual healing so Ritz could find her way to God.

Randolph Jordan went up, too. Tracee had called him the night before, inviting him to the service. He had gladly accepted her offer because he had so much on his heart.

He needed to confront his father about his father's thirty-plus-year-old lie without hurting his mother. He also had to meet his sister . . . again. He needed prayer for the fantasies he had about having sex with his sister. Granted, when it happened, he didn't know she was his sister. But now that he did, he was disgusted with himself. He was disgusted with the whole situation. He cried on his way to the altar. Randolph wasn't the only man crying at the altar.

Four people away, kneeling on the edge of the altar, was Ivan Richardson. When he had outed Edwin on Ritz Harper's radio show, he thought he would feel better. He didn't. He felt as bad as he had ever felt in his entire life. He couldn't shake the sadness, the self-loathing. All of the bitterness and anger he had been harboring against Edwin all of those years had ended up consuming him.

You reap what you sow.

Edwin's sermon that day touched him. Ivan felt guilty and convicted. He needed to see Edwin and ask for forgiveness. He no longer wanted to ruin Edwin—in fact, he had *never* wanted to ruin Edwin. Edwin had broken his heart. All he wanted was to get Edwin back.

Once he was in the presence of what Edwin had left him for—once Ivan felt the power of Edwin's church—Ivan understood why there could be no ties, no connections, no communications between them. Ever again.

This was a different world. Ivan told himself that he wished he and Edwin could somehow remain "friends," but deep down, Ivan knew that could never be. He loved Edwin too much to just merely like him.

Today, Ivan was finally ready to face his demons and to face himself. The walk to the altar felt like he was traversing the length of a football field. He was nervous and scared. He kneeled with his head bowed and he shut his eyes, squeezing out the tears.

At the same time, Edwin was making his way down the large number of people at the altar. He placed his hands on their heads and said silent prayer with them. He asked God to grant them peace and to come into their hearts and allow them to have a stronger relationship with Him. He asked God to grant them strength to overcome whatever was troubling them and to find the faith to follow whatever it was that God wanted them to do.

Edwin came to Ivan and he paused. There was something familiar about that bowed head. He hadn't seen this man in this church before, but he knew him.

He placed his hands on the man's head and prayed. When he was done, Ivan looked up, tears streaming down his face. He stared at Edwin and their eyes locked.

"I'm sorry," Ivan whispered.

Edwin froze. *Ivan! Dear Jesus, Ivan!*

"I am sorry, too, Ivan," Edwin managed to say. "I forgive you. Will you forgive me?"

Ivan buried his head in his hands and cried like a baby.

Ivan understood.

To understand all is to forgive all.

Except, maybe, when it comes to a certain New York disc jockey named Ritz Harper.

26

After church service at Faith Baptist, Randolph didn't want the day to end. He felt uplifted and bold in spirit, and he wanted to be with Tracee. She was simply so beautiful to behold. Today was the first time he had seen her in something other than casual wear. She wore a blue print wraparound dress, which fit snugly enough to show off her runner's physique. Her calf muscles were smooth and taut, allowing her to forgo stockings. She wore a three-inch navy-blue, open-toe shoe. She had her hair out, curls hanging to her shoulders, framing her face. Tracee even had on makeup—which she didn't need, but it enhanced her beautiful features. Randolph was completely smitten.

He wore a suit—one from his days in corporate America. It was perfectly tailored, and he sported a natty shirt and a perfectly tied Brooks Brothers necktie.

As the two left the church together, some congregants couldn't help but marvel at what a striking couple they made. Randolph made the first move.

"Do you want to grab something to eat?" he asked.

Church was harmless, Tracee thought, but "something to eat"? That was a *date* in her book. She toyed with saying no. But her stomach (and maybe some other body parts) betrayed her, and she blurted out "Of course" before her mind had a chance to stop her.

They had driven to Harlem in separate cars. Tracee had Ritz's Aston Martin. She didn't want Randolph to have to pick her up. Besides, she was staying at Ritz's. Ritz would be getting out of the hospital soon, and Tracee would be there to make sure there was a smooth transition for her friend. Tracee thought it would be awkward for Randolph to come to Ritz's house.

They found their cars and agreed to meet up at the Original Pancake House in West Caldwell, New Jersey. Randolph lived in Parsippany off of Route 46. The Original Pancake was way better than IHOP. It was one of the few places that served fresh-squeezed juices and turkey sausages in addition to healthy oat bran pancakes. Tracee hadn't been able to work out much since coming to New York. The least she could do was watch what she ate.

It was about a forty-five-minute drive over the George Washington Bridge to Route 46, to Route 23. Tracee drove in near silence, with just the hum of the powerful engine and her thoughts. She thought about how much she was starting to connect with Randolph and how strange that connection was, considering that he was Ritz's brother. She also thought about how and *if* she was going to tell Ritz. This was a tougher secret to keep than the one about her aunt's health. Tracee easily justified keeping her concerns about Aunt Maddie's health from Ritz. Ritz was fighting back from near death herself. An emotional blow like that, so soon after recovering, could be too much.

This secret was another story altogether. It was complicated—*very* complicated. Did Tracee want to tell Ritz the truth? She reasoned that perhaps the news of Randolph being Ritz's brother should come from Aunt Maddie. Aunt Maddie had told Ritz about her mother's death so many years ago. So she was the logical one to tell Ritz about her brother's life.

But Aunt Maddie didn't have time for that drama, with all that she was going through. Tracee knew that the responsibility would eventually fall on her. But the longer Tracee waited to say something, the more trouble it would be when she finally did. What made it even scarier was that Ritz had expressed feelings for Randolph that were anything but sisterly. She thought he was fine; Ritz even talked about conquering him.

Tracee remembered how crazy Ritz had acted when he stopped by to see her and she didn't want to see him because she didn't feel she was presentable enough. Ritz didn't want to see him unless she could look her sexy best. How in the world could Tracee tell Ritz, "Oh, by the way, that sexy dude that you want to sleep with, well, he's your brother! And oh, yeah, I kind of like him myself!"

Tracee was hoping that someone else would bail her out. Perhaps Randolph should do it? No, she couldn't put that on him. She sure wished she had a friend to talk to about this dilemma—Tracee would have been on the phone within seconds to tell her best friend about this wonderful man whom she was falling for. Under normal circumstances, Ritz would be really happy for her. Ritz had been making jokes for months about how Tracee was practically a nun—as in not getting *none*.

"Girl, how long has it been?" Ritz asked her one night when Tracee was three months into her vow of celibacy. "Look, you got seven more months of this celibacy shit and I'm having you committed. It ain't natural for a woman to be celibate—especially not for that long! Your coochie's going to get dry and grow cobwebs!"

They had laughed. Tracee didn't disagree. She thought that it would be nice to be in a relationship again, but it would have to be the right one—and she was starting to believe that the "right one" might be Randolph.

When she was with Randolph, she felt alive. Her coochie was anything but dry when he was around—quite the contrary. But that would have to be something she would keep to herself, too—for now.

She got to the Original Pancake House before Randolph, thanks to Ritz's Aston Martin and Tracee's daydream driving. He pulled up a couple of minutes later. She was waiting for him at the entrance. The place was packed, as it always was on the weekend. They took a number and sat in the waiting area near the Ms. Pac-Man and Galaga machines.

"So why don't you have a girlfriend?" Tracee blurted out. She was not usually that forward.

Randolph looked startled.

"Um, well, my last relationship didn't go so well. I caught her in bed, in *my* bed, no less, with one of my friends," he said. "She said she was tired of me spending so much time working and not with her."

"Wow!" was all Tracee could say.

"No. It was a blessing. I blame myself for being superficial. I met her in a club, and man, could that woman move her body, which was incredible. . . ." Randolph caught himself. "Sorry."

"Why apologize? That's the truth, isn't it?"

"Well, yeah, but I don't want you to think I'm some sort of ho."

"I think you're a man, and it's normal for a man to be turned on by a sexy woman," she said. "That just makes you human."

"I'm working on that part. The human part. That's the part that gets me in trouble," he said. "I almost lost it that night and wanted to kill her. But something stopped me. I went on a drinking binge, barhopping in New York on a Saturday. When I was done, I ended up in front of Times Square Church. I thought it was fate. I went in, still tipsy, with a hangover looming. The message I got that day, though, changed my life. It was then that I decided to do some pruning. I cut off all of the people who weren't right in my life—which was just about everybody."

Tracee smiled. She wasn't used to men being so open and real.

"So tell me more about your parents."

Randolph visibly winced. This wasn't a subject he wanted to talk about.

"I'm struggling with that topic right now," he said. "I'll be honest, Tracee, ever since I found out about Ritz being my sister, I have been so confused about everything. It feels like my whole childhood was a lie. My father projected this perfect family image to the world—including my mom and me. He was a pillar of the neighborhood—hardworking, churchgoing. My mom was the perfect homemaker, very soft-spoken, very loving. They seemed like the perfect couple. It was fun growing up in a house with them. They gave me everything I could possibly want.

"Then to find out that my dad, my hero, had a daughter behind my mom's back. I mean, what kind of man walks away from a beautiful little girl? I have to deal with that, Tracee. Everything I believed in feels fake now. What would you do if you found out that someone you loved and looked up to your entire life wasn't the person you thought they were?"

Tracee looked at him. She knew exactly what he was talking about, more than he knew.

"Your childhood wasn't a lie," Tracee said. "It was what it

was. You can't question yourself. Parents don't always do what they're supposed to do. They're human. We put so much faith in them. It's like they're gods and can't do wrong. Most of the time they do things because they believe it's for our own good. You have to forgive your dad, talk to him, and somehow get him to talk to Ritz. A Jordan family reunion might be in order."

"Get him and Ritz together? I'm trying to get to the part where *I* can talk to him about it. I wasn't thinking about him reuniting with Ritz. How do you think she's going to take it?"

"She's not," Tracee said. "She'll probably cuss him out and tell him never to speak to her again. But you know what—I think that's part of her problem. She lost her mother when she was ten and never knew her father, and I believe that Ritz has been spending her entire life trying to prove that she matters—that she doesn't need anything or anyone to make it. But the truth is we all need someone."

"Even you?"

"Yes, even me," Tracee said, smiling. "Especially me. Why do you think I'm trying to build a strong relationship with God? I would rather know that the one who has my back is the One who created the world. I have been so let down by people. Rand, people will let you down—that's the truth. God never will. I don't put my faith in any man."

"You can depend on *this* man," Randolph said, grabbing Tracee's hand from across the table and squeezing it gently. "I'll never let you down, Tracee, ever. If I say I'll do something, I will do it. If I make a promise to you, I'll keep it. Always. No exceptions to the rule."

Tracee felt tingles shoot through her body. She looked into his eyes and knew that he was sincere.

"Tracee, I hope I'm not being too forward, but I really like you," Randolph said. "After my last girlfriend, I decided I would wait until I found the right woman. I wasn't going to waste any more time going from woman to woman. I was waiting for someone special, someone who loves God, someone I could spend the rest of my life with. Well, I think I've found her. Yep, I think I've found her!"

Tracee was speechless. She loved the way he had spoken those words. He hadn't said them in some deep, intense, "heavy" way, like something out of a corny Hollywood melodrama. No, he looked and sounded like a little kid who had just run downstairs on Christmas morning and was marveling at the presents under the tree. But Randolph wasn't marveling at a present. He was marveling at *her*.

She wanted to do something crazy, like tell him she loved him. But she was scared. How could she tell him something like that? She hardly knew him, but she felt she had known him forever. It was too confusing. It was too soon. So she said nothing.

"I know we just met. I know I haven't known you long," Randolph said. "But it doesn't take all day to recognize sunshine. I see you. I see who you are. And I know I can love you. Do you think you can love me?"

Tracee was sitting in front of a man handpicked by God, a

man she could not have constructed if she went into a store and bought a kit and built him from scratch.

"I guess what they say is true. When God does something, He goes way beyond what you could possibly imagine," Tracee whispered under her breath. She didn't intend to say it loud enough to be heard, but she couldn't hold it in.

"What did you say?" Randolph said, smiling. He heard her.

She looked at him and smiled back. He was still holding her hand; he had it cradled in both of his.

Tracee didn't have the words to express what she was feeling, so she leaned across the booth and kissed him. It was a kiss that came from her soul. Randolph saw that soul. Randolph felt that soul. Randolph *knew* that soul—and he always had, if the truth be known. He just hadn't met it until he met Tracee.

He kissed her back. Perfect. Perfect. *Perfect.*

27

After seeing her aunt and her sad condition, Ritz was more determined than ever to reclaim her life, or at least life as she saw it. Her aunt's disease proved the old adage: Here today, gone tomorrow!

Ritz wasn't focusing on anything *real*—like the *real* possibility of an infection, or the *real* possibility of a relapse that would make her an invalid, or the *very real* possibility that a crazy killer would be coming back to finish the job he botched.

Ritz was obsessed with only one thing—getting herself back on the air. Ritz needed "the air" the way everybody else needs oxygen.

She sat up in her hospital bed, which she now *hated* (first line of business when she got home: a $10,000 water bed!), and dialed Ruff.

"Okay, look, I am coming home in a couple of days," Ritz said as soon as she heard Ruff's voice—no hello, no small talk, just the assumption that he was there, ready to take her orders. "I expect to be back on the air next week, or you will be hearing from my lawyers. And don't give me any 'You need to recuperate' bullshit. I have recuperated more than everybody at Sloan-Kettering put together. I'll worry about my health. You just set up your end. I'm ready to come back, and I am coming back with a vengeance! Do you hear me?"

Who the fuck does she think she's talking to? Ruff thought.

But "Yes, I hear you" was what actually came out of Ruff's mouth.

He wasn't afraid to go toe-to-toe with her. He was the program director. He ran the station. He would always win that fight. But he was getting fed up with her. Ever since she had gotten into the spotlight—and *he* was the one who had put her there, let's not forget that—she had turned into a demanding diva bitch. She was rude, obnoxious, and nasty. That part Ruff could handle with no sweat. Actually, he loved her spunk and take-no-shit attitude. Ritz Harper was a strong woman. You had to admire that about her, whether you liked her or not.

It was her sense of entitlement that irked him, like she was doing him, the station, and the Free World a favor by plopping her big ass in a seat every day, doing her show, and oh, yes, by the way, getting paid millions of dollars a year in the process.

In radio, everyone could be replaced. In media, anyone

could be replaced. Just ask Star Jones Reynolds—sitting all high on her throne at *The View* and then, "Blammo!" she was out of there. Hell, *Oprah* got fired from an anchor spot early in her career. Somebody actually *fired* Oprah Winfrey. Howard Stern had been fired when he was bringing in super ratings and ad revenue. Even Wendy Williams had been pushed out of New York at one time while her ratings were red-hot.

It happens to the best of them. You can be good, profitable, with good ratings, and still get the boot. Radio was a business, and there were certain things that "the suits" did not tolerate—not for all of the money in the world. Ritz didn't realize it, but she was dancing dangerously close to the abyss.

In the end, WHOT management decided to give Ritz everything she demanded. A crew was sent over to her home to set up in her basement to broadcast the show. It was soundproofed, and she had the proper mic and headset to make it sound like she was right there in the studio.

Chas's takeover plans were now dashed, so he was back in the fold like he never left, jawing in Ritz's ear about what they should do and how they should do it. But Ritz wasn't following his guidance anymore. He would have to follow *hers*. She didn't trust Chas to have her back. He wasn't there for her when she was on the brink of death. He had a lame excuse about trying to rescue the show and keep the station from replacing her. Chas told Ritz he was the one who convinced Ruff how much they needed Ritz. But she wasn't buying it completely.

Ritz decided it was her car and she would be driving it from now on. She had the license and she was going to use it. Chas's place now was to sit in the backseat and shut the fuck up.

We'll see how this plays out, he thought. He might have to be a brownnose for a while, but that was okay. He knew about power and Ritz didn't, which is why, in the end, people like her always lost. Chas recalled one of his favorite maxims:

Always be good to the people you meet on the way up, because you may need them on the way down.

Chas thought of that old adage, then he thought of Ritz Harper, and then he laughed, and laughed, and laughed.

☆ ★ ☆

Ruff had reluctantly given in to Ritz's demands. The hard part now was convincing his general manager that he had made the right move.

"Ritz is being released from the hospital, Miss Gogel. She is demanding that she do the show from her home." Ruff made sure to put a little extra emphasis on the word "demanding."

"Well, what are you going to do?" Abigail said. "I have an idea. Why not shoot her again? Just walk up to her, like those people in *The Godfather*, and say, 'Sorry, Ritz. This is business, not personal,' and then boom! Problem solved!"

Ruff bit his tongue. "We can either fire her now and eat

the final two years on her deal, which is a lot of freaking money, or we ride it out," he said.

"We can't pay out that kind of money! Isn't there a 'morals clause' in her contract? We have to set her up so we can get her out of here and not pay a dime. Get on it. Today. Actually, wait a day or two. I'd like to think of something that would really cook her goose. But it's got to be good. Don't bother making her out to be 'gay.' Nobody cares about that anymore. I have to watch *Maury* this week and see what's hot these days."

Ruff swallowed his tongue again. "I'm working on it, believe me. This Michelle Davis is a star, and she's the kind of star who would have made your grandfather proud. We can build a lot around her."

Ruff loved Ritz, but he had been a proud radio pro for more than twenty-five years and he hated what radio had become. Back in the day, someone like Lenny Bruce was one thing: He was poking a finger at hypocrites and trying to get people to get real with themselves. His "shock" had a purpose in a 1960s America where people were still drinking from "colored" and "white" water fountains, women were still expected to stay home, barefoot and pregnant, and married couples couldn't be shown sleeping in the same bed on TV.

Ruff felt that today's radio was just too much. Shock to enlighten and educate was one thing, but shock for the sake of shock was just a bunch of banal, boring bullshit. Now there were radio hosts who were getting people to have sex in churches, while others were having strippers on as guests and getting them to touch each other and talk about their vaginal piercings. There was one host who was giving young girls instructions on how to perform oral sex. There was another who had threatened to urinate on another host's little girl. It was sick stuff. Ruff used to be proud to say that he worked in radio. Now he was ashamed.

But he was a businessman. He knew that if he couldn't beat them, he had to join them. Ruff's job was to get ratings, and Ritz brought ratings. Ritz also brought drama, which brought even *more* ratings. It was a vicious merry-go-round, and Ruff wanted to get off that ride right now.

But just as he was thinking of walking away from the radio game, cashing in his pension, and retiring to Arizona, Ruff met Michelle Davis. More important, Ruff *listened* to Michelle Davis.

He had listened to her and was spellbound. Yes, Michelle Davis spent time going through all the *Page Six* and *Rush and Malloy* stuff, but her message was to rebuke it, not to emulate it. Michelle Davis did not admire celebrities, or politicians, or business tycoons, or rap stars, or anyone else who might be on the cover of this week's *People* magazine.

Michelle Davis was a bit strange. Michelle Davis admired teachers.

At the end of her show, just before signing off, Michelle had said: "And remember this, folks: Do you *really* need a friggin' Cadillac Escalade?"

After the broadcast, Ruff was excited again—for the first time in a long time—about his profession and its possibilities.

Listening to Michelle reminded him how he had felt the first time he heard stereo FM after listening to tinny AM on a little Zenith transistor radio for so many years. It was like hearing a new world.

Now he had to figure out how to get rid of Ritz Harper. No one had pulled harder for her to make it back than Ernest Ruffin.

Now he just wanted her to go away. *C'est la vie*.

You reap what you sow.

Ritz sat in the passenger seat for the drive to Jersey. Tracee was handling the Aston Martin like James Bond in *Goldfinger*.

"I never thought I'd say this, but I think this car is worth every dollar you spent on it," Tracee said. "This is a fabulous ride. It's practically driving itself. How are you feeling?"

Tracee drove up to the gate at Ritz's Llewellyn community. There was a policeman stationed there in addition to the guard. Tracee had to show identification. She was relieved to know that there was around-the-clock protection. There was still a killer on the loose, and if Detective Pelov was right, he would try again. Tracee hoped he was wrong. She drove around the winding roads inside Llewellyn and pulled into Ritz's circular driveway and down the back way to her three-car garage.

"It's good to be home" was all Ritz said.

Tracee helped Ritz out of the car. Inside, Ritz's home was full of fragrant bouquets, cards, and balloons from fans and coworkers. They were everywhere. Ritz's cleaning lady was there to let the deliveryman in and they arranged the flowers beautifully.

Tracee helped Ritz climb the stairs to the enormous master bedroom.

"All the flowers were delivered from the station," Tracee said. "They were bombarded with well-wishers. Beautiful, huh?

"I also took the liberty to hire an industrial cleaning service to do the rugs and windows—the things Maya doesn't do on a regular basis. I wanted to make sure that when you came home everything would be perfect and you wouldn't have to worry about a thing."

Ritz appreciated the flowers. She couldn't wait to get back to her gardening hobby, and she was looking forward to getting her hands back in the soil.

"You are staying here with me, aren't you?" Ritz asked.

"That was the plan, wasn't it? You promised me some fun, and we're going to have some fun! I brought some DVDs from Blockbuster."

"Oooh! That sounds like *so* much fun," Ritz said sarcastically. "Did you get any porn? My favorite porn actor is Dick Johnson. He's so long, he can stick it in his ear. But I just read an article about him. Now he really wants to direct."

"I can see your sense of humor is still intact," Tracee said, and laughed. "What? You want to go to the club or something? Girl, you better lay down so you can be one hundred percent better. That's why I'm here. You're going to watch movies and you're going to like it. Look, I got *Which Way Is Up?*"

"That Richard Pryor movie? You have got to be kidding."

"And I got you *Baby Boy*, too!" Tracee said.

"Now you're talking!"

Ritz was tired. She did need to lie down. She wanted to settle in to being home. She also was restless. All she could think about was getting back on the air.

"Where's my phone?" Ritz asked.

"Why do you need a phone?" Tracee asked. "You need to relax. There's plenty of time for talking on the phone."

"I have to call Chas and Ruff and see what the plan is for the show," she said. "I have to call Jamie. I told her that she would have to move in when I got back on the air. I have to get this place ready and have everything in place. Maybe I will be back by Monday."

"Can you just concentrate on taking care of yourself? Think about resting and recuperating."

"There will be plenty of time for rest when I am dead," Ritz said. "I've had enough rest. Right now, I need to get back. Look, I almost died. Some fucking bastard tried to kill me and take all of this away from me. I am going back on the air as soon as possible. At the very least, I need to know what's happening with my show. Can you please bring up my radio from the kitchen?"

Ritz had a Bose iPod system in her bedroom, but she rarely listened to the radio when she was home. She didn't need to.

The only show she cared about was hers. Ritz needed to know what was going on during her time spot. She knew a few things. One, her audience wasn't necessarily *her* audience. Anyone with talent, a gimmick, a plan could come along and snatch them right from her grip, as she did to Dr. Biff. While Ritz believed she was different, special, and that what she had built was so unique that no one could top it, she wasn't a dummy. She knew that by and large, people are fickle and they can be easily swayed.

Here today, gone tomorrow. She had to get back soon.

It was twenty minutes before three, and Ritz didn't want to miss one minute of the show. She had missed enough being in the hospital with the controlling-ass nurses and doctors who kept jabbing her with needles and keeping her from being on top of her game.

Ritz had spoken briefly with Chas before leaving the hospital. He'd said something about a fill-in. That was something Ritz never wanted. A fill-in was a potential replacement. She had hoped they would continue with *Best of* shows until she was ready to come back, but Chas said that the station management wasn't having it. They wanted new material, not "Golden Oldies."

"Tray, hurry up with the phone and the radio," Ritz yelled.

"Yessssss, master," Tracee yelled back. She knew this was going to be a trying time, responding to Ritz's every need now that she was back up and running. Ritz was lucky that Tracee loved her and was willing to put up with the Diva Act.

Tracee found Ritz's phone and radio.

"Now, don't get used to this service, Missy," Tracee said. "Don't think that just because you're infirmed, that I won't jack you up if you get out of hand. Where's my belt?"

Ritz looked at her nails. They needed to be done, stat, like they said at the hospital. She also wanted to order that water bed.

"Thanks. That reminds me—Jamie's supposed to be here after the show. Can you get her room ready? I think you've been on vacation for—what, almost a year and a half? Maybe you need to get back to work. In fact, I need some things from the store. Be a sweetie and run to the store for me."

"Ritz Harper, you're a trip!"

"Can you get me some cherries, and some tea, and some reefer?"

"I don't think they sell reefer at ShopRite," Tracee said. "But I can run to Whole Foods. I think they have some hemp. You can chew on that. You still smoke that stuff? Dang, girl!"

"'Judge not . . .' and you know the rest, Miss Holy Roller," Ritz said.

"Whatever! Now, you said you wanted cherries and what else?"

"Some tea, and if you do go to Whole Foods, get me some of those organic chocolate-covered almonds. Yummy."

"Can you have chocolate?"

"What am I, a dog, now? Listen, Nurse Betty, don't come in here trying to mess up my fun. Get to work!"

Tracee rolled her eyes again.

"Look, I'm not working because I'm retired, and I retired

to do exactly what I wanted to do," said Tracee, smiling at the thought. "You sound jealous."

"Oh, no! I can't wait to work again!" Ritz said. "Yeah, I'm going to get Jamie here. Girl, you have to see her boyfriend. He is sexy!"

"Watch that, Ritz," Tracee said.

"I already did!"

"Uh-uh! No you didn't!" Tracee said in disbelief. "Plus, I thought you had your eye on that electrician."

"Oh yes, thanks for reminding me of that hunk of a man," Ritz said. "He's a real challenge, and you know how I like challenges. I have to break him down. But Jamie's man— now, that brother broke *me* down. I swear, if I think hard enough, I can still feel the soreness, if you know what I mean."

"Girl, that soreness is probably the result of one of your gunshot wounds. And stop playing. You didn't actually sleep with that girl's boyfriend?"

"No, I fucked him," Ritz said. "There was no sleeping involved at all."

"I can't believe you! Does Jamie know?"

"I hope the hell she doesn't!" Ritz said. "That's part of the fun—knowing she doesn't know, and watching him squirm around me. I can't wait to have her invite him over one evening. I'm trying to figure out how I can get him alone for like fifteen minutes. Or a half hour. Or an hour. He knows how to hold it down, Tray! Damn. That man can *last*! I haven't seen anything like it!"

"Okay, Ritz, you're officially back," said Tracee, slightly disgusted. "But if you want my advice, which you never do, I would say: Stop it. That's just wrong. I mean, come on, Ritz. You cannot be having fun at that poor girl's expense. It's not right."

"You're right, Reverend Remington. Forgive me, for I have sinned! But I came three times!"

Tracee ignored her friend's sarcasm.

"And, and . . . I have something else to tell you. The electrician? He's kind of off-limits, too."

"What?!" Ritz said. "Don't tell me you fucked him! You did? How was he?!"

"No! God no! I mean, what I mean to say is that yes, I do like him. I like him a lot. But there's more."

"What?" Ritz folded her arms, ticked off. How in the world could Tracee dare to like a man that *she* had dibs on?

Tracy stared at her friend. She was about to unload the biggest "bomb drop" of all time. Things would never be the same again.

"Ritz," she said, trying to keep her voice slow and steady. "Please listen. Aunt Maddie thought that this should come from me. Ritz, Randolph is your brother."

"What??? What the FUCK are you talking about??!!! I don't have a brother!!!!"

"Yes. Yes, you do. You have a brother and a father. Randolph's father is Ritchie Jordan."

29

"My brother?!"

Ritz looked like she had been sucker-punched. The air went out of her healing lung and she had a hard time catching her breath. Thousands of thoughts went racing through her mind:

Where has he been all of these years?
Why did he leave us alone?
Where is he now?
How could he start another family?
What kind of man is he?
Do I even want to see him?

"My brother? My father? What the fuck?!" Ritz stammered.

"Well, I guess he had sex with your mother. And then he

had sex with Randolph's mother, and the three of them pro-
duced you two."

Tracee was trying to bring some lightness to the atmo-
sphere, which was getting heavy, *real* heavy. But Ritz was not
amused. She gave Tracee a stare that looked like pure rage.

But Tracee knew her friend well. Underneath the rage was
hurt, bewilderment, and, above all—curiosity.

"Okay, okay. Sorry for trying to be funny. I guess it wasn't
the right time for that. Randolph is going through it, too. He
had no idea. Apparently, his father cheated on his mother
with your mother. No one knew. And I don't know what happened when he was over here fixing your Jacuzzi, but it
weirded him out."

Ritz blushed. She remembered back to how seductive she
was . . . with her brother.

*Yuck! I almost screwed my brother! Maybe I should go on the
fucking Jerry Springer show!*

"I don't want to talk about that," said Ritz. "I'm not sure if
I can even see Randolph again. And how did you two get so
close that he's sharing his feelings with you? What's really going on, Tracee?"

"Nothing! Nothing yet. Like I said, I do like him. And I
think he likes me, too. We got close all of those times you
turned him away at the hospital. We went to church together
and we have been talking. When he found out he was your
brother, he had no one to talk to. He still hasn't said anything to his father—your father. He doesn't want to hurt his
mother. "

"*His* mother?! What about *my* poor mother!" Ritz screamed. "*She* was the one left holding the bag, struggling to raise me by herself. That motherfucker left us high and dry. At least Randolph got to grow up with a daddy. At least his mother had a husband. She didn't have to hang her head in shame, looking like some loose girl with no morals. *Fuck him* and his mother, and *especially fuck* his father. Fuck the whole fucking family!"

"So you don't even want to see your father? You don't want to tell him how you feel?" Tracee asked. "I think it would be good for you to do that. Even if you cuss him out. You can't hold on to these feelings, Ritz. It will destroy you. And we know how you hold grudges. It's not good. You have to let it go. You have to find closure."

"I am finding closure," Ritz said. "I'm shutting this shit down. I don't have a father—end of story. That's closure. And I don't want to see that electrical motherfucker around here, either!"

"Why are you acting like this? Randolph is just as much a victim as you are. He didn't do anything."

"He was born. That was enough!"

Actually, Ritz didn't give a damn that the man was her brother. That was the anger she allowed to show. She was severely pissed that Tracee would *dare* to look at a man Ritz coveted. *She* was Ritz Harper. Tracee Remington was just . . . some retired person.

The real anger, the real, deep-down pain, though, was about her father. Ritz was going to bury that. She'd heap a bunch of junk on top of it and dare it to breathe. She was not going to feel that. She was going to hang out with her old buddy KIM and keep it moving. She didn't have a father, and that was that—case closed. Next!

"Okay, Ritz. I will respect your wishes," Tracee said calmly. "I won't talk about Randolph. But you must know what a special man he is. You might find out that it's nice to have a big brother."

"I don't need a big brother or a midget brother. I got me!"

"We all need somebody, Ritz. Even you."

"You don't know what the fuck you're talking about. And you definitely don't know who you're talking to!"

Ritz was going into her industrial-strength, completely-over-the-top Diva Mode, her ultimate defense mechanism. Hurricane Katrina? That was a summertime sprinkle. Hurricane Ritz was about to rage through anyone and anything that *dared* to confront her. She would level them. She would destroy them. She would get even.

Why, Daddy?

Deep down, in a place in her soul that she could never, ever acknowledge, Ritz could hear a little girl named Ritgina—a little girl who once knew all the state capitals—crying out that question.

Why, Daddy?

Ritz was about to explode. She would not, she could not, listen to that little girl. That little brat better go away, *fast.*

Tracee was speaking to her. Tracee better watch out!

"You're right, Ritz," Tracee said. "When I look at you and all you've been through, I don't know you. I'm not sure if you even know yourself. I pray to God every day that you will wake up and see the changes you need to make. You're not happy. I *know* you're not happy. Yet you keep doing things to make sure you *won't* be happy. You're self-destructive. You push away everyone and anyone who might want to love you. You aren't the Ritz I met. Or maybe you *are* the Ritz I met so many years ago. Maybe you haven't changed. Maybe I have."

Hurricane Ritz was going to unload on Tracee and blow her into next week. Maybe *that* would make the little girl go away.

"You sure have, with your judgmental self!" she raged. "And all that 'God' and 'church' shit! You know what? You and God can *kiss my ass*. And you know what else, Tracee? Get the fuck out of my house!"

Tracee stood in front of Ritz, stunned. Ritz's face was contorted and changed into something ugly, something Tracee had never seen before. She couldn't find any words to say, so she said nothing.

She went to the guest room. She packed the few things she had put away. Then she called a cab. She didn't want to call Chas, and definitely not Randolph. That would take too much time. She had to get out of Ritz's house—now.

She would go back to her loft in Manhattan and pack that place up. Then she was going to swing by the hospital to say good-bye to Aunt Maddie and Uncle Cecil. After that, she would invite Randolph Jordan over for a little going-away dinner, then she would return to the peace she had created for herself in Winter Garden, Florida.

She was going home.

Ritz had stormed off to her room, slamming the door with the little energy she had. She did nothing when Tracee's cab arrived. She heard Tracee knock at her door, but she didn't respond. She heard Tracee tell her that she loved her and that when Ritz was ready, she would be there for her. She heard Tracee say good-bye. She heard the cab drive off.

Then she heard the little girl's voice again, the little girl's voice that would not go away:

Why, Daddy?

Why, Daddy?

Why, Daddy?

30

Ritz set up her radio, propped up her pillows so she could sit comfortably for four hours, and got ready to tune in to her show. She grabbed her phone to call Chas. She hadn't really spoken to him since the shooting. They needed to have a heart-to-heart.

Chas picked up on the second ring.

"Chas here!"

"It's Ritz," she said in a matter-of-fact, you-should-be-expecting-my-call manner.

"Oooooh! Diva! How does it feel to finally be home? You know I've been busy trying to keep your show together, girl. It's not the same around here without you. It's a lot more work. These amateurs they have filling in are giving me fever," said Chas.

"So they invited that Fox News bitch back," Ritz said.

"What's up with that? I thought there was going to be some sort of rotation until I return next week. How does this bitch get to sit again? I don't like it, Chas. I don't like it one bit!"

"I don't like it either. It was Ruff's call. He said he wanted to see if she could handle the whole week."

"What?!" Ritz was fuming. "The whole fucking week?!"

One of Ritz's major stipulations was that she didn't want anyone sitting in her seat. And if someone had to fill in, they better not fill in for long.

"Okay," she said. "You have to sabotage that bitch today. I don't care what you do. But she better fall on her face, Chas. I am so serious! Look, I'm ready to go back on the air tomorrow. You tell Ruff to call me. Because I'm ready now! Where's Jamie? Send her over here as soon as the show is over. Let her know her room is ready now. She can come over after the show. Make it happen, Chas. I know you can."

"Sure thing, diva. Sure thing," Chas said, hanging up the phone. The last thing he wanted to do was set things up for Ritz to be back on the air. But he had to keep up appearances, at least for a little while.

☆ ★ ☆

Ritz turned on her radio. It was six minutes after three and she could hear her theme music playing. Then there was this voice. Very sultry, very authoritarian. Very strong.

"Is that Michelle Davis?!" Ritz said to herself. "How is that bitch filling in for me? She's not even a radio person. Who the fuck does she think she is? Who the fuck did she fuck?"

As Ritz listened to the first hour, she learned who Michelle Davis was. Not only was she a budding radio personality, she was handling Ritz's show with aplomb, taking it in a direction Ritz could never take it. Ritz was heated.

"I always told Ruff that I never wanted a bitch sitting in my seat," Ritz said to herself again. "How the fuck did this happen?! This has to be her last day in *my* seat!"

Her hands were shaking with fury. She turned the radio off after the last caller was telling Michelle how well she was doing. Ritz couldn't take it. Not one person said how much they missed Ritz. That wasn't good. Once your audience gets hijacked, you're done. She dialed Ruff's number. The phone rang three times and went to voice mail.

"Ruff, this is Ritz. I'm home. I need to talk to you ASAP. Call me back!"

She hung up. Ritz's brain was clicking. She had to come up with a plan. Monday was too late. The damage would be thoroughly done. But if she couldn't do anything until Monday, then when Monday did come, Ritz had to come back with a bang. They had to forget this Michelle bitch and remember what they loved so much about Ritz.

She had to call Chas again and plan out one of the best shows of her life.

31

Tracee opened the door to her loft and breathed a sigh of relief. Even though she hadn't called the loft her home for more than a year, she had quickly gotten reacquainted with it. She knew this is what a home was supposed to feel like. Her simple wood floors and soft light never seemed more warm and inviting. She realized just how sick she was of animal prints and the color black, all of which seemed to match Ritz's dark soul.

She walked over to the window in her living room that went from the floor to the ceiling and watched the parade of yellow cabs scramble through the streets below, and felt at peace with herself and her home. She realized for the first time that she loved her loft. The unrest she associated with it and New York City had really existed only within her, not around her.

Despite the nasty departure from Ritz's and the heated words exchanged, Tracee's nerves were not shaken. She decided she was going back to Florida, but not to escape. She was going back because she missed the weather. She was going back to Florida, but she knew now that New York was also home. First thing in the morning, Tracee would call her realtor, Spencer Means, and take her loft off the market.

Hesitantly, Tracee picked up her phone. It was late, but she had to make the call. She tapped the contacts bar on the bottom of the screen. She thought how ironic it was that Randolph's name was perched right above Ritz's on her contacts list.

Randolph picked up on the second ring.

"Hello? Tracee?" He recognized her number from the caller ID.

"Hey," she said.

"I didn't expect to hear from you tonight, at least not while you were in the same house as Ritz," he said, propping himself up in his bed on one elbow. Hearing Tracee made all his senses come alive; he was wide awake.

"I hope I didn't wake you, but I just wanted to say goodbye, because I am heading back to Florida."

"Wha-what?!"

"But . . . the good news is I'm not leaving for good. I'm keeping my loft. So I'll have good reason to come back as often as I want."

"Wait! Hold up! What do you mean you're leaving?" Randolph sat up immediately. He swung his legs out from under his covers and sat on the edge of his bed. He wasn't prepared for this, and he couldn't hide the disappointment in his voice.

"What are you doing right now?" Tracee asked.

"Nothing."

"Good. Please come over to my place. I want you to see it. And I want to say good-bye to you in person. I am trying to get a flight out tomorrow afternoon."

"Of course, Tracee! Give me your address and I'll be right over," he said.

Randolph hung up the phone, put on a pair of navy-blue sweatpants, a T-shirt, and a pair of Timberlands. He grabbed his cell phone, car keys, and wallet and headed for the door. Maybe he could convince her to stay just a couple more days. He didn't want her to leave.

☆ ★ ☆

Tracee's loft was sparsely furnished, so it took no time to make it immaculate and inviting for Randolph. She opened the fridge to see only two bottled waters and some baking soda. But if he was hungry she could order something, or they could walk to one of the numerous stores around the corner.

She didn't know whether she should change the sheets. She smiled to herself. What was she thinking? She allowed herself to explore that for a moment.

The phone rang. Even though she was expecting his call, the phone startled Tracee out of her thoughts.

"Hey, Tracee. I'm downstairs. What apartment?"

"A-17." Tracee quickly glanced around the apartment, making sure everything looked just right. A person's home revealed so much. She unlocked the door and left it ajar and stood by the window, wanting to take in all of Randolph's body language as he entered her space.

He opened the door fast, as if he had been there before. He didn't look around, as she assumed he would. His eyes went directly to her. He walked over to her at the window and held up both hands as if to say, *What's up?!*

He reached out and grabbed her hands.

"Tracee, why are you leaving? Why so fast? What happened? Was it something I said?" It was Randolph's feeble attempt at humor, which wasn't his forte.

"Ritz and I had this big fight, and she told me to get the hell out of her house," Tracee said. "Actually, she didn't use the word 'hell.'"

"Wait. Ritz threw you out?"

"Yeah. She told me to get out. She was angry about a lot of stuff that's not right in her life. I guess it was just easy to dump all of her crap on me. She's great at doing that to people who happen to care about her.

"What I do know is that I will be there for her if she ever needs me. But I will not be one of her flunkies who tolerate her abuse. But I didn't call you here to talk about that, Rand. I called you to say how wonderful you are and to say that I hope this is not a permanent good-bye."

Randolph led Tracee to her simple chocolate, leather sectional that she had found at Huisraad, a store in the Mall at Shorts Hill. Where most leather sectionals are masculine, Tracee managed to find one that was feminine, with curved armrests and extra-soft leather. Randolph interlocked his fingers behind his head and looked around in amazement. As an electrician, he had been in many homes—some of the most magnificent, and some of the crappiest. Tracee's was one of the most exquisite he had seen. It wasn't just the architecture, which was unique in a loft space. Most lofts have a steely, industrial feel, but this one actually felt like a warm, cozy home. Tracee didn't have much furniture, but the furniture she chose and the colors she used and her selection of art pulled it all together.

She took him by the hand and gave him the grand tour. She enjoyed showing him the artwork on the walls— all of which was original. Her pride and joy was a piece by this hot artist Bernard, who had a shop in South Orange, New Jersey. It was an incredible oil painting of a little girl in a yellow dress with Afro puffs. She'd bought it one day while she and Ritz were hanging out on South Orange Avenue.

Tracee led Randolph upstairs and they continued the tour. The upstairs was just as beautiful as the downstairs.

They sat on the top step of the staircase.

"You really have great taste," Randolph said. "That bathroom sink upstairs is unique. And where did you find those lights? It's like you have stars in the ceiling. I wish I had done that for you."

"I get a lot of ideas from watching HGTV. But since I was a kid, I have kind of been into home improvement and decorating. I love it. Maybe I'll take it up when I decide to come out of retirement. I am planning on redoing this place when I come back."

"Yes, let's talk about you coming back," he said. "Better yet, let's talk about you *not* leaving. Okay, so you had a fight with Ritz. But what's back in Florida for you?"

Tracee didn't want to dredge all of that drama up again. She just wanted to sit there with Randolph. She was so near to him, and she now could really see his face. She knew he was handsome, but he was *really* handsome up close. Most men had hair bumps, or a crooked tooth somewhere. This man had no flaws—or least none that Tracee could see. Randolph sat there, waiting for an answer.

"My house is in Florida," she said. "And I have a few things to take care of with that. Part of my life is there."

Randolph looked at Tracee's face as she spoke. He wanted to take in everything about her. He loved the way she smelled, but there was no expensive "scent" lingering from her. It was just her body chemistry, and he couldn't explain it, but it smelled so much better—*so* much better—than anything he had ever smelled from a bottle.

He ran his hand across the side of her face, tucking some of her soft curls behind her ear.

The place where his hand touched her face left a searing hot spot. It was like electricity shooting through her body.

Tracee knew immediately that she had it bad for him. She was trying to tell him what happened earlier that evening, but she couldn't remember anything she had said once he touched her hair.

Tracee stood up. "Randolph, can I get you something to drink? I have water and I have . . . water."

He burst out laughing. "Thanks. I think I'll have some water."

Before she was able to get up and go get the water, Randolph reached out and grabbed her hand.

"Trace, look, I want to just say that I don't want you to leave. I have more of a bond with you than I've ever had with anyone. You can't go back to Florida. Not yet. I'll get the water. You just sit and relax and think about it."

Randolph went to the fridge and pulled out two bottles of water. He handed her one as he settled on the step right below her.

"Rand, you're making this very tough for me," Tracee said.

"Good! Now stay."

"I want to go and just clear my head. I feel like I've been through a battle and I need to get better, get strong again. I lost my best friend—twice. I am going to lose a woman who is like a mother to me. Maddie doesn't have much time left. I know that. How brave she is. And she loves Ritz so much— so much.

"Then there is Uncle Cecil. Seeing him breaks my heart. He's in the middle of it all. What a good man, what a strong man. It makes me want to strangle Ritz, to see how callous and immature she has been to them.

"Then there is a murderer out there somewhere, who may try to kill Ritz again. It's too much. I just need a little break," Tracee said, as tears started burning her eyes.

She didn't realize how much of a bundle of raw nerves she was. Her Christian walk was getting tougher and tougher these last couple of days. She got up from the steps and went down to the couch, where she put her face in her hands and sobbed.

Randolph sat down on the couch next to her and pulled her over so that her head rested on his lap. He watched a tear fall into her right ear, and while he wished he could do something to make her feel better, he knew the best thing to do was listen.

Neither of them spoke. Tracee looked up at Randolph, and he looked at her. The quiet between them was long but not awkward—it was a beautiful, comfortable silence. The feelings they had for each other lingered in the air, certain and understood. Tracee reached up and gently guided his mouth to hers. She kissed him lightly.

Randolph could taste the salt as he kissed her eyes before letting his tongue part her lips gently. Tracee kissed him, forgetting everything that pained her soul. She didn't remember when they stopped. She seemed to doze off and float into a place of peace.

Later, when she opened her eyes, Randolph was behind

her on the oversized sectional, holding her, hugging her. She had never felt more secure.

At three in the morning the phone rang, waking both of them. Tracee recognized the number from the hospital.

"Hello?" Tracee knew the familiar voice, and there was something terribly wrong with it.

"Tracee, this is Uncle Cecil. Maddie's gone, Trace. Maddie's gone."

32

Ritz had Jamie running around like a chicken with its head cut off.

"Jamie! Get me my diet Pepsi! I need it now!" she yelled from her basement studio. "I also need more pillows. I need more pillows!"

Jamie rolled her eyes. She was *thisclose* to quitting for the third time since she started working with Ritz. The contempt for her boss was overflowing. Jamie was grateful for the promotion to assistant producer and the regular paycheck. She was grateful for the opportunity to learn so much. But she was getting tired of being treated like a peon by Ritz. And being at Ritz's place practically twenty-four/seven was wearing very thin on Jamie.

However, there was a part of her that was okay with keeping so busy. At least she didn't think about Derek.

"Jamie!" It seemed like a constant rant coming from Ritz, who seemed to need something every second. Jamie was waiting for Ritz to start ringing a bell to beckon her.

She brought down the drinks and the pillows and set up the computer so that Ritz could communicate with Aaron and the studio. Jamie also made sure that all of the ringers on all of the phones were turned off. Ritz was going to sound like she was in the studio even if she wasn't. There would be no distractions.

She had the television, tuned to CNN *Headline News*, on mute. She kept that on for breaking headlines. Ritz wanted to make sure she was on top of everything. If the world blew up, she would know and immediately let her audience know.

Jamie did a test with the studio to make sure that Ritz's voice levels were perfect and to make sure there was no feedback, which could be really distracting. It was two minutes to showtime. It had felt like two eternities since Ritz Harper was on the air, and she was nervous.

"Let's rock and roll!" she screamed into her headset before her theme music started. Ritz was a bundle of excitement.

On Air.

"I mean, whose side are you on, Jen's or Brad's?" It was a cheesy question, Ritz knew. It was an old and tired topic, too. This she also knew. But it was one that Ritz could guarantee brought some calls once she put her spin on it. She needed to get back into the flow with her audience, so she decided to take an easy path and work her way in slowly the first hour. She had a trick up her sleeve for hour two that would definitely make headlines. But for now, it was Jen and Brad.

"Oh, this is so tired," Ritz continued. "Are we still talking about this? Who cares, really? I definitely don't. But I've been away for a while and you all haven't had the pleasure of getting my analysis of the whole affair. So get your pens and some paper, and Mother is going to break it all down for you right now and tell you what really happened. And what's great about this is that it's a lesson for all you women out there.

"Okay, ready? Jennifer Aniston never wanted to have a baby with Brad Pitt, because she knew somewhere deep inside that he was a low-down, dirty cheat who couldn't keep his wanker in his pants for more than twenty minutes. I will list his girlfriends—the women who came before Jennifer Aniston. You will need a couple sheets of paper for this. Okay. He dated Robin Givens—remember her, Mike Tyson's punching bag . . . I mean wife? That gives him a little extra credit, because it shows that he's an equal-opportunity screwer. He went out with Gwyneth Paltrow (the two starred together in the movie *Seven*). He bedded Jill Schoelen, who was his costar in some unmemorable movie called *Cutting Class*. Nine months later he was on Juliette Lewis, another costar in another lousy NBC movie called *Too Young to Die*. The strangest thing is that whomever he dated he started to morph into. *He starts to look like his girlfriends.*

"Juliette Lewis was going through this 'goth,' freakish look, and Brad looked weird, just like her. When he was married to Jen, his hair was ashy blond, like hers. Now it is

Angelina Jolie dark brown. I find this a little odd, but hey, to each his own, right?

"He also dated Julia Ormond, his *Legends of the Fall* costar. Then he met and married Jennifer, *then* he met, screwed, and had a baby with his *Mr. and Mrs. Smith* costar, Angelina Jolie.

"Now, I understand why Jennifer Aniston got with Brad. Ladies, can I get a witness? And all you 'how you doin's' out there, holla! He is the sexiest man in the world—of any race or ethnicity. Tell me you haven't seen those naked pictures of him in *Playgirl*?! Yummy. Okay, okay . . . he ain't packing like the brothers. But I suspect that there is more 'there' than meets the eye. I have seen things go from dud to 'whoa buddy!' and surprise the hell out of me before. I think Brad Pitt is in that category. But to tell you the truth, just looking at him and that freaking perfect body makes me not really care whether he's packing or not. Um, we're going to have to go to commercial or a song or something while I get me some ice water. And I'm not drinking it, either!"

Aaron took his cue, played "Ay, Papi Chulo!" and started a commercial set.

Ritz smiled to herself. She was in her element, getting back in the game. She would prefer to be in the studio, but at least she was on the air again. She didn't know whether she would be rusty, whether the audience would be ready for her to return. There were a lot of unknowns. But the display on her laptop computer that was loaded with "assistant producer software," giving her a direct link into the studio's computer, showed her that the audience was still there. She hadn't even asked a real question and every line was lit. Her adrenaline was pulsing through her body. Being on the air again was better than any drug or any man she had ever put in her body.

She was getting pumped up for the bombshell she was going to drop in hour two. She wanted to take her audience by surprise. It involved a rapper and his wife. It was a story that came to Ritz simply because she was Ritz. People in hospitals, nurses and even doctors, folks who worked in hotels, waiters and hostesses in restaurants—were all her informants. She was able to get the dirt on just about anybody, because people wanted to be in Ritz's good graces. She realized she didn't need Chas as much anymore; she had more than ten million Chases spread out over thirty-plus states.

One of her informants gave her a nice, juicy tidbit that nobody knew. Ritz was back. She was back and more explosive than ever. She had gotten a tip about a Grammy-winning singer who was checking into a health spa, but it was actually rehab. The music world hadn't had this kind of scandal since they found out that Whitney was on crack—er, um, cocaine (because "crack is wack!"). This multiplatinum singer, who had endorsements with the Disney company, was known to be a bit eccentric, showing up on the red carpet in outlandish outfits. Now Ritz was going to tie her strange behavior to cocaine abuse.

Ritz also had more dirt on Hardcore, the former hot rapper who used to be one of Tracee's artists. Ritz had outed him last year and ruined his career. The worst thing for a hardcore gangster rapper was to be rumored to be gay. Now she had him linked up with another famous rapper. It was so juicy, Ritz could hardly wait until Wednesday to drop that bomb.

Or maybe, I'll save this until Friday, she thought. *Give them something to talk about over the weekend.*

No thought was given to Tracee. Ritz wasn't trying to think about anything but her mission ahead—to be back on top.

Jamie was trying to settle in. She spent most of the time in the room Ritz had for her. It was a beautiful bedroom, bigger than her own, with the most comfortable bed she had ever slept in, but Jamie wasn't comfortable there.

Ritz appreciated the company. She felt safe having someone in the house. But Jamie was very standoffish. She was sad. Ritz would ask her about it, maybe. Actually, she thought more about Jamie's boyfriend and hoped he would stop by some night to see her. She didn't know how she would do it, but Ritz had to have Derek again.

After another successful show went off without a hitch, Jamie retired to her room after asking if Ritz needed anything. Ritz was exhausted. The adrenaline of being back on the air had carried her over the last few days, but it was all catching up with her.

"I don't need a thing, Jamie," Ritz said. "Just some sleep. I'm turning the ringer off on the phone. I don't want to be disturbed. I'm going to be out for the next twelve hours."

"Okay, see you tomorrow," Jamie said, closing Ritz's bedroom door behind her.

☆ ★ ☆

The knock was so hard, it jolted Ritz out of her sleep.

"What the fuck!" she said, looking at her clock and seeing that it was a little after three in the morning.

The knock came again.

"Yes!" Ritz screamed. "What the fuck is the matter?!"

Jamie cracked the door.

"I am sorry to bother you, but it's your uncle. He's on the phone," she said. "He needs to speak with you."

Ritz grabbed the phone next to her bed.

"Uncle Cecil?" she said, hearing the click on the other end as Jamie hung up the phone in the guest room.

"Ritz? Ritz?" he stammered. "It's your aunt. She's gone."

Ritz was stunned. She knew her aunt was sick, but Ritz never imagined her dying—especially not dying before she had a chance to see her one last time. Ritz had been meaning to get by to see her again. She was going to go earlier in the day, but she was all caught up with getting back on the air. She was caught up with her life. She figured she would have time.

Ritz meant to have a heart-to-heart with Aunt Maddie. While they had reconciled, there was still so much more to say. And she knew Aunt Maddie wanted to talk to her about something, about Randolph. About her father.

But the truth was, Ritz didn't really feel like talking—not about that. She also didn't like seeing her aunt like that. She didn't like how weak Maddie was, how sick she was. After spending so many weeks in the hospital herself, Ritz just didn't want to go back there—not even for her aunt. But it was over now.

"Uncle Cecil, I'm sorry," said Ritz. "Don't you worry about a thing. I'll be right there. I will be right there, Uncle Cecil. I'll take care of everything."

Ritz hadn't driven since she got out of the hospital, but she found her keys on the island in the kitchen, started up her Aston Martin, and headed to the hospital. She would take care of everything. Aunt Maddie would have a queen's send-off. Ritz was not going to spare a single expense.

33

Ritz sat in the front pew, wearing the fiercest black Moschino dress she could find with such short notice. Actually, Chas found it, pulling a favor with one of his stylist friends who worked at Saks Fifth Avenue. It was her first appearance in public since the shooting, and while it was not the way she envisioned her public debut, Ritz wanted to make sure she represented herself well. She expected the newspapers and television outlets to be there in droves. And they were—with reason.

It had been quite a week for Ritz. She kicked it off with her first week back on the air. Through a tip from a listener, Ritz found out that the wife of Phaze One, a giant in the rap world, who crossed over to make hit movies and even a successful run in a television sitcom, had been diagnosed with cancer. It was such a big secret that family members of Phaze

One's wife were unaware of her condition. But Ritz Harper knew, and she put it on blast. She attempted to sound concerned for the woman, who was a beauty in her own right and a top model before she married Phaze One. Ritz sounded really sympathetic when she talked about the "poor woman's hair" falling out.

"That chemotherapy just ravages the body," she said with a pang of recognition, as she thought of her own aunt suffering the same fate. The irony. But Ritz wouldn't let it go. This was one time when perhaps her own circumstances would call for her *not* to go where she was going. But once again, her desire to be *the* baddest bitch alive made her ignore the obvious.

"The doctors say she has less than six months to live," Ritz continued with her monologue, directing Aaron to play sad music in the background. "Phaze One, I hear, already has a replacement waiting in the wings, though. Hmm. Now, that's really sad."

That was when she went too far. When Ritz came back from the break, the studio notified her that she had a call waiting for her. It was Phaze One.

"Oooh, goody," Ritz said with glee. "Put him on!"

"But, Ritz, I don't know about this," Aaron said. "He sounds pretty angry."

"That's even better!"

Chas, who was in the studio, couldn't help but smile. *That damn Ritz is too much!* he thought. But he was loving every minute of it. He forgot the adrenaline rush that went with what she brought to the table. No one else was like Ritz. No one.

Aaron looked at Chas, his last line of defense. And Chas gave the nod to put Phaze One on the air.

"Boy, you better be quick on that button," Chas said to Aaron. "I know we are going to need every one of those seconds on that six-second delay with this one. You better not miss a beat, Aaron."

"I got this! I got this!" Aaron said.

Ritz welcomed everyone back.

"And I hear we have a special guest on the line. Phaze One, welcome to the Ritz Harper Excursion. First, let me tell you how sorry we are to hear about your wife," Ritz said, putting on the sweetest voice she could muster.

"Bitch, miss me with all of that bullshit!" he said. Aaron was able to bleep out the "bullshit!"

"Who the fuck do you think you are?! You are talking about a woman who has a family and children. Do you not give a fuck who you ruin?! What is up with you, bitch? What is your problem?!"

"I'm sorry, Phaze One, I don't understand. How did I ruin anyone by reporting the truth? Your wife does have cancer, doesn't she?"

"And why is that any of your fucking business?"

"Well, you're a public figure. And people are concerned. They want to know."

"You are the foulest bitch in the world. Didn't you already get shot once? You must care more about your fucking career than you do about your life, bitch. Keep my wife's name out of your mouth! If I hear you talking about me or mine again, I'm going to fuck you up!"

With that, Phaze One hung up. Ritz was not deterred or afraid. In fact, she was defiant.

"I'm looking here at Phaze One's wife's medical report. It looks as if the cancer has spread. I am going to ask the audience to say a prayer for Mrs. Phaze One. She's going to need lots of it. We're going to a break, but the phone lines are open. I want to hear from you."

The threat against Ritz and Ritz's bold disclosure about Phaze One's wife's cancer made national headlines. There was even talk of a possible arrest of Phaze One for the threat he made on the air. On the heels of the shooting of Ritz Harper, any threat was to be taken seriously.

Ritz didn't stop with that. On Tuesday, she took it up a notch. She announced the firing of a talk-show host. The problem was that the host had no idea she was being fired. Ritz got the memo from a secretary of one of the bosses at the network, spelling it out. The secretary was an avid listener and a rabid fan, and she wanted to do anything to help Ritz. Ritz called the talk-show host live on the air and informed her of the firing. It caught the talk-show host completely off guard. She was embarrassed and she, too, ended up hanging up on Ritz—but not before Ritz humiliated her and made her cry. It was great radio. Ritz was so happy to be back on the air.

Ritz didn't have any guests that first week. She wanted to be just her reconnecting with her audience. She wanted them to feel what they had missed the couple of months she was out of commission. But she was back. By Friday, it was official. Ritz Harper was the queen of the airwaves. When she was one hundred percent, she would tackle television next. She heard Delilah Summers was going to have her own show on CNN in the fall. Ritz had to top that.

Before she could get ready for that next move, though, she got that call in the wee hours of the morning from her Uncle Cecil. Ritz was sad about her aunt's passing, but she was also mad.

Just when I get back on my feet, something comes along and tries to knock me off, she thought.

Ritz sat in that first pew with a stone face. Her Uncle Cecil sat beside her, sobbing uncontrollably. She put her arm around him. Aunt Maddie might have preferred a church funeral. But Ritz was handling everything and she didn't belong to a church. She secured the Frank E. Campbell Funeral Home. Cuban salsa singer and megastar Celia Cruz had had her funeral there a couple of years back.

It was a storied place, known for catering to the stars. The Frank E. Campbell Funeral Home held the wake of actor Montgomery Clift back in 1966, and more than thirty-five years later, it was the viewing place of singer Aaliyah, who died tragically in a plane crash before she was able to see her twenty-third birthday.

Frank E. Campbell, which was located in the upscale Upper East Side at Madison Avenue and Eighty-first Street, held the funeral of Luther Vandross as well as The Notorious

B.I.G. Ritz didn't attend either of those funerals, but she stood outside with the crowd that day. It was quite a scene. Her aunt may not have been a star or a celebrity, but Ritz was. And this funeral was as much about Ritz as it was for Aunt Maddie. Ritz needed to show her strength and her courage in the face of adversity. She was going to emerge victorious.

The beautiful, wood-laced first-floor chapel was filled to capacity with Ritz's fans, station personnel, acquaintances—sycophants of Ritz—and the news and entertainment folks. There were also several plainclothes police officers at the funeral home, including Detective Tom Pelov. He had been keeping a low profile but was very much on the case. It was stumping him, with very few leads. But he was determined to find some clues and capture the person or persons who tried to kill Ritz Harper. He was certain they would strike again.

Derek was there, wearing dark shades, dark khakis, and a simple blue dress shirt. He had waited outside on East Eighty-first, waiting for everyone who knew him to go into the funeral home. He didn't want to see Jamie. He was there for Ritz. He wanted to give his condolences. He took a seat in one of the last pews, near the door. About twenty rows in front of Derek was Tracee. She had already delayed her plans to go back to Orlando. But after finding out about Aunt Maddie, she was definitely sticking around. Maybe Ritz would reach out to her. At the very least, she would be there for Uncle Cecil. Tracee had visited Aunt Maddie just two days before she died. Aunt Maddie was very weak, but they got to really talk. Tracee confided in Aunt Maddie about her family and about her walk with God. She read some scripture and they talked about how Tracee had given her life over to the Lord. Aunt Maddie had never made that commitment and feared it was too late. Tracee told her it was never too late. She grabbed up Uncle Cecil and the three of them prayed, and Aunt Maddie, who had been baptized when she was twelve but never really got into church much, accepted Jesus Christ as her savior.

Tracee loved Aunt Maddie as if she were her own aunt. It was her pleasure to foot the bill for their hotel and hospital stay—even though that became another fight with Ritz, who insisted on paying her back every cent.

Tracee sat there, tears streaming down her face, heart heavy. Randolph Jordan sat next to Tracee, holding her hand. Randolph was just getting to know the Robinsons and really liked the relationship between the two. He also was very fond of Aunt Maddie's strength, courage, and brutal honesty. He was looking forward to getting to know his new family a whole lot better. But now he wouldn't have that chance. He squeezed Tracee's hand gently, letting her know he was right there.

Jacob Reese sat in the middle of a pew in the middle of the chapel. He wanted to blend in. He knew he wouldn't get another shot at Ritz today. But he wanted to get a good look at her. He wanted to see her up close. He wanted to remember her the way she was before he killed her. This time, for good.

☆ ★ ☆

Ritz stood tall at the door of the funeral home, flanked by armed undercover cops. Her uncle was at her right side, trying to be strong. People came by and wished her well.

Tracee and Randolph gave Uncle Cecil a big hug. Tracee didn't want to let go of Uncle Cecil as the two cried with their heads together for several minutes. Ritz rolled her eyes so that no one could see her. She knew Tracee was sincere, but she was jealous of the closeness Tracee had with her family. While Tracee and Uncle Cecil had their moment, Ritz tried not to make eye contact with Randolph, who stood off to the side, giving them their space. He wanted to say so much to Ritz. He had these visions of her coming to his parents' house and meeting their father. He had plans of being the brother she never had. But Ritz didn't look like she was open to any of it. Randolph was going to respect that. Tracee said Ritz would come around when she was ready. He would wait for that time to come. In the meantime, he was there. He didn't say a word, but he let his presence be felt.

A teary-eyed Tracee came up for air, still holding Uncle Cecil's hand. She looked at Ritz and gave her a big hug, too. Ritz returned it, but it was fake, complete with a dismissive pat on Tracee's back. Ritz would keep up appearances and wouldn't make a scene, but Tracee wasn't having it. She had so much to say to Ritz but knew that this wasn't the right place or the right time.

"We need to talk," Tracee said. "And we will."

Ritz gave her a phony smile and nodded. Tracee and Randolph left. The burial would be in Virginia. Uncle Cecil decided he wanted his wife home, buried next to her own sister and mother. He would have a private burial with a few of Madalyn's friends down there.

Derek was one of the last people to come through the line. Ritz smiled when she saw him. She didn't expect to see him. It was a pleasant surprise. He shook Uncle Cecil's hand and said he was sorry for his loss.

He was about to say the same to Ritz, who leaned over and whispered in his ear, "I want to see you tonight. Come over around nine."

Derek didn't respond. Should he go over? He wanted to see her, too. He had been wanting to see her, too, but he was too cool to ever show that. Derek almost didn't show up, but it was the best excuse he would ever have for seeing Ritz again.

Jacob Reese was a few people behind Derek, who left the funeral home to take care of some business before hooking up with Ritz later in the evening.

He walked up to Uncle Cecil and gave his condolences, and then he hugged Ritz as if he knew her. It was a strange hug, and Ritz felt it. She gave him a fake smile and a thank-you. But she couldn't shake the strange, creepy vibe she had gotten from that man.

Who is he? she thought. *A fan?*

Detective Pelov noticed something, too. He decided to discreetly follow him and find out exactly who he was.

34

Derek called when he got to the gate.

"It's me," he said. "Jamie's not there, is she?"

He had to ask. While he didn't think Ritz would invite him over with Jamie staying with her, he couldn't assume. Ritz was a wild bitch; she might get off on seeing Jamie hurt. It was sick, but that was part of what he loved about Ritz—she was a cold, ruthless bitch who didn't give a fuck. But there was the other side that made her even more intriguing. The way they fucked that night, he could not shake it. He couldn't forget it. He wanted her again and again and again. Just thinking about that night made his dick hard.

"Of course she's not here! I gave her the night off. I told her I had a lot on my mind with my aunt's funeral and I wanted to be alone," said Ritz, sounding a little insulted.

"I had to know because when I get there I'm going to

fuck your brains out and I don't want any distractions," he said.

Ritz's clit jumped and she hung up the phone.

"Sir, you can go up." The guard handed Derek back his ID, which passed the police check.

Derek drove up the winding road to Ritz's house, his palms sweaty on the wheel. He didn't know why he was so nervous. He chalked it up to anticipation. It was months since they were last together—before the shooting. He had wanted to see her after she was shot but couldn't justify it to Jamie or himself.

"I was nothing more than a lay," he said to himself. "I don't matter to Ritz Harper."

But apparently he did. At least a little. There was a sense of urgency about Ritz's request to see him and to do it at her aunt's funeral. Derek cleared his evening schedule, took care of all his business, and made sure he was there before nine.

He pulled into the circular drive and parked around back so that his Jeep wasn't visible from the street. He walked up the drive and rang her doorbell. It was like she was waiting at the door for him the whole time. She opened the door immediately, wearing a lavender silk Victoria's Secret robe and nothing else. Her double Ds were spilling out.

Ritz practically pulled Derek inside the door, closed it behind him, and started kissing him. He eagerly kissed her back, as he started taking off his clothes. He lifted her up and slammed her against the wall opposite the door. He pulled down his pants and didn't get his shirt off all the way. But he fucked her right there in the foyer. It was a hard, violent, passionate, mindless fuck that had both of them exploding in ecstasy at the same time.

There were no words exchanged, no foreplay, and no condom.

35

Three days before the funeral, Jacob Reese parked on Main Street just outside of Llewellyn, the gated community where Ritz Harper lived. He noticed the unmarked police car at the gate and the officer checking everyone going into the well-to-do community. He cased the area for three hours. He didn't want to stick around too long. Jacob didn't want to be noticed. He took notes.

The next day, he took the Midtown Direct New Jersey Transit train from Penn Station out to the area early. He got off at the Main Street in Orange exit and walked the mile and change up the hill to West Orange. It was better on foot, to get a sense of the neighborhood and to find vulnerable areas where he could get into this place and take care of business. Every day, Jacob was getting more and more desperate. He had spent a lot of money in anticipation of collecting his quarter-of-a-million-dollar bounty for killing Ritz Harper. Since the bitch was still alive, he was not only in debt, he was on the brink of homelessness and hunger.

Before he had set out to kill her the first time, he didn't really care about Ritz Harper. He didn't know her, rarely listened to her. She was just in the wrong place at the wrong time. Because she lived, it now became personal for Jacob. He hated her for living. He hated her for making his life miserable. He blamed her for all of his troubles. Ritz Harper had to die for real this time. His plan had to be foolproof. He watched four officers who took shifts watching the community. There were also four guards who sat at a booth near the gate.

There has to be a back way—there has to be a way into this fortress, Jacob thought.

He walked around the grounds, and sure enough there was a way into Llewellyn—over the fence on the back end of the grounds. No one was patrolling this area. *Where there is a will, there is a way.* It wasn't barbed wire, it was just very high and awkward iron fencing. But it wasn't too hard for Jacob to get in.

Jacob noticed that at night there was a car that patrolled inside the grounds. That, too, was new because of resident Ritz Harper. But the car didn't start patrolling until after midnight. Jacob had time.

Ritz's exact address was given to Jacob by the person who had hired him to kill Ritz. He waited until the sun went down to scale the fence. People didn't just stroll around Llewellyn.

You either lived there or you were there to commit a crime. Pedestrians stood out in this community. The only people on the streets were folks with baby strollers or dogs, and everyone knew everyone. A strange face—even one as nondescript as Jacob's—would definitely be noticed and acted upon. Jacob had to stay out of sight.

He found Ritz's street with relative ease. He hid in her bushes on the back side of her grounds.

"Damn, this bitch is living very well," Jacob said to himself. "I'm living like a dog and she's got a fucking three-car garage. And look at the size of this house—it's a fucking mansion!"

He slinked around to the garage area to see if there was an entrance he could gain without being noticed. He was certain she had an alarm, but would it be on if she was home? He noticed a light on the third floor.

"That must be her bedroom," he said.

The garage door opened and Jacob ducked into the brush. A Jeep came out of one of the spaces; he could see a beautiful shiny Aston Martin parked in the garage, too. He squinted to get a glimpse of the person driving the Jeep. It was a woman. And she looked familiar. Jacob expected someone to be staying with Ritz. He actually expected there to be surveillance of her home by police. Maybe there was. He wasn't going to the front of the property; it was too risky. Whatever he did, it had to be from the back.

He noticed that the garage door took about a minute to close completely; perhaps he could slide under the next time it opened. Just then he spotted a window on the second floor. Maybe it was open. He would climb up the side of the house and try it. Before he was able to do it, another Jeep pulled into the driveway. It parked just outside the garage door. Jacob would have to wait to make his move.

36

Detective Pelov left his car in the parking area at the tennis courts near the front of the gate. It was dark and the gas lighting provided little illumination.

It must be nice living in such a great neighborhood that you don't have to worry about lighting and crime, he thought. Detective Pelov rarely found himself in these quaint little hamlets with their gaslights and no sidewalks. Very few crimes happened in places like this. He hoped that there would no crime tonight, either. But his senses were telling him that there was going to be a problem.

He walked for what seemed like forever to Ritz's house. There didn't seem to be much activity, which he was relieved about. As he was approaching the front, headlights headed up the driveway. He ducked behind some evergreens in the front of her home. It was a Jeep. He jotted down the license plate number to check later.

After the Jeep pulled out, he thought he heard some rustling around the back of the house.

Pelov unhooked the snap on his holster and removed the safety on his Glock. He tiptoed down the driveway, staying close to the house. Ritz had that dumb gas lighting around her home. She wanted to keep with the theme of the neighborhood, but Pelov could barely see anything in the dim, worse-than-candlelight glow.

Out of the corner of his eye, he caught a glimpse of a figure. It was a man, attempting to scale the side of Ritz's house, climbing a trellis.

"Freeze!" Pelov said, grabbing his Glock with both hands. "Police!"

Jacob lost his footing as he reached for his own gun. As he fumbled for it, Detective Pelov didn't wait. He released three shots, center mass. Jacob hit the ground, headfirst with a sickening thud. If the bullets didn't kill him—and they certainly did—the fall would have.

Detetive Pelov took out his cell and called the front gate, requesting the office to come to the crime scene. He also called headquarters.

"I think we got our killer," he told his captain. "This case is finally over."

Hardcore sat in one of the plush leather recliners in his theater room in the dark. His home was the only thing left from his failed career; he'd paid for it in cash. But with twenty-one thousand in taxes due each year (and rising), he would have to hustle to cover it. He dreamed of a comeback, but nobody wanted a hardcore gangster rapper who was rumored to be gay.

In rap, particularly the brand of rap that Hardcore did, which was the 50 Cent, Shyne, C-Murder kind of rap, you couldn't even have a hint of gayness. Not only was it *not* accepted, it could get you hurt. It was right up there with being a gay reggae star (even though there were one or two who definitely were).

You could be a drug dealer, you could be a wife beater, you could be a rapist, you could even be a murderer and have a successful rap career. But gay? That was a kiss of death. And while there were a few rappers who were rumored to have been gay—they were softcore rappers who had pop, crossover hits and did family-friendly movies. And those were whispers. What Ritz Harper did to Hardcore was put him on blast.

"That fucking bitch!"

Ever since the day that Ritz Harper outed him on her nationally syndicated talk show, his life had not been the same. He had been dropped from his record label. That part he actually could have overcome. It was his real life—his childhood friends, who were distancing themselves; his mother, who had to face her church friends—that really hurt him. While his mom never said a word, Hardcore could see the pain and disappointment in her face.

His mother had to endure a lot of disappointment at the hands of Hardcore—whose real name was Fred Samuels. He had been shot twice. He dropped out of high school when he was sixteen. He never went to class anyway. All he kept in his school notebooks were rhymes—pages and pages of rhymes. Hardcore didn't understand how a high school diploma was going to make him a millionaire. He wasn't working in a fast-food joint like some of the nerds in his neighborhood—mostly immigrants. Black kids didn't work at fast-food joints in Bed-Stuy. They made fast money on the streets.

Hardcore loved the danger of selling weed and cocaine. He loved the nightlife and the camaraderie of his boys sharing their dreams and hustling until the wee hours of the morning. That also broke his mother's heart. But he didn't care then. He thought, *At least I've never been locked up.*

And to his credit, Hardcore was never arrested, while most of his street hustling buddies were snatched up one by one. He considered himself smarter than they were. He always knew when Five-O was about to come and he managed to stash his stuff and never get caught.

For some, going to jail was a badge of honor. Hardcore saw it only as being dumb and sloppy. And he was proud that he was able to avoid that hassle. He was also proud that he saved his money. He didn't buy a whip and put expensive rims on it. He didn't buy platinum and diamonds. He didn't go out and get grills or a whole lot of clothes. He saved his money.

So when his break finally came, he wasn't impressed with the three-hundred-thousand-dollar contract. He didn't feel the need to blow it all on dumb stuff, because he had already disciplined himself to not want those things.

Hardcore's break came when he was able to corner Charles Suitt, who was a vice president of A&R at the time at Universal Records. Charles was at a club scouting new artists, and Hardcore got him in the doorway as he was leaving. He spit a few bars of a rap he had created after the first time he was shot. Charles was impressed. He invited Hardcore up to perform for the bosses and he was signed on the spot.

The head of urban music, Jean Briggs, pushed Hardcore's music until it was number one in the country, which was a lot for a gangster rapper. In the music business, success can come if you're talented. But more often than not, it comes because there is someone very powerful behind an artist pushing their music. And at the time, there was no more powerful person in music than Jean Briggs. She made it happen, and Hardcore was experiencing success he never imagined. He had enough money to buy a Mercedes and a mini mansion in a nice neighborhood in Bergen County, New Jersey. He had an indoor pool, a game room, and a theater room. He paid for it all with the millions he made off the sale of his first CD. He paid cash just in case.

He made a nice friend, too, in Tracee, who was a record label executive. She was Jean's number two and became Hardcore's mentor. She helped school him on the game. But none of them imagined that it could all be taken down by the careless, insidious actions of one woman—Ritz Harper. In one afternoon, everything Hardcore had built was thrown into the abyss.

Hardcore was obsessed with Ritz Harper. He had dreams about killing her, choking her, and laughing as she gasped for air. He had daydreams about pulling her down a long flight of concrete stairs by her feet as her head hit each and every step. He never considered himself a violent man, but there was something about the way Ritz Harper delighted in telling the world that he was the gay rapper she was talking about that made him furious.

The worst part was that it wasn't true. Hardcore had be-friended a young artist and invited him to stay with him. He took him under his wing and wanted to give him a chance to not make the same mistakes he made. Their friendship was close enough to be misconstrued. There were very few people Hardcore could trust. He couldn't hang with his boys from the old neighborhood anymore. He had outgrown them. He didn't care. But he never expected something so innocent to cost him his career. And for his feelings to be gutted and splayed for the world to see.

Hardcore was furious at Ritz. And it wasn't just about him. He remembered how hard Tracee took it. Ritz was supposed to be her friend. But Ritz didn't even give Tracee a heads-up.

"What kind of person is she?" Hardcore asked Tracee. "Does she have a soul? How can she not care about people?"

"Yes, baby boy. She's just a little lost" was all Tracee would say. She was definitely disappointed in her friend. Then, when her bosses decided to drop Hardcore over it, it was the last straw for Tracee. She couldn't stay in an industry that didn't stick behind good people. And Hardcore was good people. *Was.*

His thoughts of revenge consumed him. He wanted to get Ritz Harper. He wanted to shut her up for good. He reached out to a studio groupie, who he knew was desperate and would do just about anything to get near the recording industry. Hardcore promised Jacob a shot at producing, and he told him he would pay him a lot of money to take care of his Ritz Harper problem.

When Jacob screwed up and didn't complete the job the first time, Hardcore was beside himself.

"Either that bitch is a cat with nine lives or that motherfucker I hired is retarded," Hardcore said to himself. He told Jacob he better finish the job this time, or else.

When Hardcore found out that not only did Jacob *not* finish the job, but he somehow managed to get himself killed, he was beside himself. Now what? Was there anything out there that could connect him to Jacob? Would someone be looking for a connection?

Jamie, who had been officially hired by the station and given a decent salary, was preparing her next move. After the drama died down over who shot Ritz Harper and after being held hostage twenty-four/seven under Ritz's rule where she daydreamed of doing violent *Kill Bill* types of things to Ritz, Jamie was ready for a change of scenery.

It was time to move on.

Jamie had learned a lot from Ritz while being tortured, and she even grew to respect Ritz's work ethic and accomplishments (which might have changed to out-and-out hate if she knew the truth about Ritz and Derek). Jamie learned that while she desired a higher salary, it was never going to be the amount of money she made that gave her the comfortable life she wanted, it would be the saving and investing of that money. Jamie started a "Kiss My Ass Fund," something Ritz often said every woman should have.

When Ritz finally stopped hounding and riding Jamie every evening at around eleven when there seemed to be no time for her to do anything for herself, Jaime would retreat to her room and read one of the many financial books that Ritz kept in her home office. For a little more than three weeks, Jaime was stuck reading books by David Bach, Jonathan Pond, Suze Orman, and Robert Kiyosaki. At first it was all she found to read, then it was the only thing she *wanted* to read. She would find herself reading the books into the early morning. It was like a light went on inside.

She managed to put every bit of advice that the books had to offer to use. She opened an online bank account that paid a high APY. She called the human resources department at the radio station and enrolled in the company's 401(k). She opened a savings bonds account at treasury direct.com, and for the first time in her life she bought stock. She bought stock with a discount online broker, Share-builders.

For some reason, the comments that Ritz spewed at her had less of an impact on her psyche. Jamie would smile because she was accomplishing her goal. She could endure anything because the bigger picture was right in front of her. She knew that Ritz didn't control her destiny, she did.

With the confidence Jamie had built, she applied for a position that even she thought might be out of her league. But she thought, *What do I have to lose?* She had a degree in marketing, only to be bitten by the entertainment bug in her senior year. The job was an associate marketing analyst for Smith Barney, one of the largest investment houses in New York City. More than a month after she applied, she was called in for an interview, which she aced. After dealing with Ritz, there was no person on earth that could rattle her. Jamie had learned to multitask at the highest level. She had also learned all of the nasty, cutthroat moves she needed to not only survive but excel in the corporate world. Jamie held the offer package in her hand and thought to herself how the bane of her existence had given her priceless life lessons without knowing it. Jaime stuffed the envelope in her bag, took a deep breath, put a smile on her face, and pushed through the studio doors.

She was buying her freedom. She was leaving the Ritz Harper Excursion for good. Jamie was starting a brand-new life.

☆ ★ ☆

Ritz, who had been back in the studio for less than a month, didn't bother to look up and acknowledge Jamie when she walked in. Ritz was too preoccupied with getting a back-ordered Fendi bag. With the shooting thing and the killing thing and the dead aunt thing behind her, she was ready to get back to her other hobby—discount shopping.

"Jamie, call the guest for my third hour and confirm the

time," Ritz barked. "I'm sick of these rappers thinking they can just do whatever the fuck they want!"

"I'm on it," said Jamie, knowing that this would be her last couple of weeks working in this gulag camp.

"Get Chas on the phone and let him know that we should be able to hit both clubs tonight," Ritz continued. "I should have three bottles of Moët chilling at my table once I'm off the stage. At each club, that is. And don't forget to invite the new head of black music over at Universal. It's important that I have a connection with all these new artists."

"Okay," Jamie said, but she didn't move immediately to get on it the way Ritz expected. So Ritz looked up from what she was doing, looking puzzled. Jamie stood before her confidently.

"Ritz, I need to speak with you at the end of the show," said Jamie, who knew that Ritz never would engage in any conversation that didn't pertain to her before she went on the air.

Ritz nodded an okay. Then she started looking in her purse for her favorite lipstick, when all of a sudden the most irritating case of heartburn came over her. Ritz knew that she needed to stay still or her pink office/studio would be splattered with a different kind of animal print.

Jamie was surprised that Ritz didn't give her a smart remark. So she simply turned and began to fulfill Ritz's many orders.

"How much time before we go on, Aaron?" asked Ritz, using one hand to brace herself as she slowly stood up.

"We have about ten minutes," he said. Aaron shrugged his shoulders, amazed that Ritz was such a damn diva that she couldn't look at her fifteen-thousand-dollar watch to see the time for herself.

I guess that thing doesn't tell time, Aaron thought. *Too many diamonds.*

Aaron's patience was wearing thin, too. He was her biggest fan, but since Ritz came back, life had been hell for him, too. She was just a bitch. There was no comedy anymore. Anytime there would be a remote hint of fun, Ritz would go on about how she "almost died and nothing is fucking funny!" That was getting a little tired for Aaron—and everyone else.

Nothing was fun about working there anymore. His crush on Jamie had waned, and she was even more standoffish *after* she was dumped by Derek. Chas wasn't around as much, and when he was, he didn't seem to be totally into it. So what was once a fun career was now just a job for Aaron.

Aaron was jarred out of his dark thoughts by Ritz, who bolted out of the studio. She ran to the bathroom, kicked open the last stall, and barely made it to the toilet seat, where her stomach flipped inside out. All of its contents landed in and around the toilet.

Ritz hovered over the seat, still feeling queasy. She knew she didn't have much time. She just hoped she had some gum in her purse. Ritz got out of the stall, ran some cold water over a paper towel, and wiped the back of her neck, her forehead, and her mouth.

"Shit! I can't be sick!" she said to herself. "I have too fucking much to do."

She'd been going at a thousand miles an hour since she came back, not going to sleep until three in the morning most nights. She needed to slow down.

As she gingerly walked back to the studio, she bumped into Chas in the hallway on his way to the studio.

"Hey, Chas," Ritz said. "Listen, I'm not going to be able to make both of those appearances tonight. Maybe I can do just one."

"Hold on, Miss Diva!" said Chas, very annoyed. "I put my word out at the clubs that you would be there. I can't have you not show up!"

"Look, I need to slow down. I feel like shit," she said. "I've been going nonstop since I got back. You didn't just almost die, Chas, it was me! Can I get a little compassion?"

Chas walked ahead of her and opened the door. As she passed by, he rolled his eyes and gave her the middle finger behind her back. But while his middle finger was still waving in the air, Ritz turned quickly. She saw it, but she wouldn't be able to acknowledge the insubordination, as she had to hurry back to the bathroom to toss her cookies again.

"One minute before we go on!" Aaron yelled out.

Ritz would make it back. The show must go on. Ritz wouldn't even hint at an illness when she got back to the studio. She just did her show and did it well, as she always did.

39

The last time Ritz Harper was in a hospital she was clinging to life, riddled with bullets. She didn't even visit the hospital during her aunt's last days, she hated it so much. Ritz hated the smell, she hated the nurses, she hated the whole scene. Sure, she got star treatment, the special private room with all of the amenities. But it was still a hospital.

This occasion, however, made it bearable.

Ritz was there doing something she never thought she would ever do—have a baby. She delivered in a room by herself, just as she wanted. There was only her doctor, a nurse, and an anesthesiologist. Yes, she was having an epidural. *All of the pushing and hollering and that natural childbirth shit is for the birds,* she thought. *I want this baby to slide out, pain free.* But even with the epidural, Ritz swore it felt like she was pushing an Escalade through her coochie. And she wasn't sure, but she thought she pushed so hard that she even shit on the delivery table.

But all of those thoughts were erased like amnesia, because all Ritz could remember before she passed out was the doctor saying, "You did great! It's a girl!"

Ritz woke up in her private room. A nurse came in, holding a little bundle in a blanket, talking about feeding time. Ritz had not planned on breastfeeding, not with her implants just getting settled after having one of them replaced following the shooting. It was bad enough that she had to mess up her figure for a few months, and God knows how long it would take before she'd be back to her diva shape. She also knew that a little nip and tuck would be in order after she fully recovered.

"Whatever God didn't do, I know some doctor will fix," she said to herself, knowing she would have at the very least a tummy tuck, a butt lift, and some liposuction around her thighs.

The nurse had no expression as she handed Ritz her baby.

"The doctor will be in in a moment to speak with you," said the nurse solemnly before leaving the room.

Ritz looked puzzled. She held her baby and a serene sense of joy washed over her. Ritz was surprised. She didn't know she would feel this way. *Unconditional love? Is this what that feels like?* Ritz realized that she had never experienced this before in her entire life.

Ritz was alone. Derek wanted to be around. He wanted to

be a father, but Ritz couldn't see herself with him. He was a drug dealer, after all. And young, too young. She had decided she would raise this baby herself. She would be there for her little girl, the way her mother was not.

"I will never leave you," Ritz said, pulling back the blanket to get a good look at her baby. It was the first time Ritz had really gotten to see her daughter. She stared into a face that, less than an hour into this world, had a striking form. Ritz was looking into a mirror when she looked into the face of her baby girl, who had the same pretty, smooth complexion, a few shades lighter. The little girl looked to have the beginnings of the same deep dimples that Ritz had.

Ritz saw herself for perhaps the first time in her life. She saw herself in a way she never expected. There was an innocence in this baby that Ritz could hardly identify with, but it seemed to crack open a window inside of Ritz. It began to melt that solid-ice-cold heart Ritz had developed over the years. Ritz knew for the first time that she never knew love until this day.

She was madly, wildly in love with her baby.

40

Ritchie tucked the address into his jacket pocket. He gave himself one final once-over before leaving the house. He wanted to look perfect, and he did. He was in his early sixties, but he didn't have a single wrinkle. His dark, chocolate complexion was smooth and strong. His mustache was salt-and-pepper and his hair, which he kept real low, was a beautiful silver. The contrast of the white hair and the dark skin made him even more handsome.

In his day, and even this day, he was the kind of man who would turn heads. But there was only one woman he had his sights on—his daughter.

He hadn't seen her since she was a baby. Ritchie didn't have many regrets in his life. He considered himself a good citizen. He had a beautiful wife, a great son of whom he was very proud. He was fairly successful—had the house, a nice car, and all the trappings of someone who lives well.

But there was one blemish on an otherwise stellar record.

He had his reasons for not being there for his baby girl—his namesake, no less. He even secretly followed her career and fame with both pride and shame. But who was he to judge?

He thought the hardest conversation he would ever have would be with his son. And it was tough. Randolph felt betrayed and lied to. And he was. His primary concern was his mother, but he was also shocked to learn that she knew—she knew it all.

Randolph said he needed time to process it all. And he was taking his time. He had a new woman in his life and he wanted to start a new life free from drama, lies, and chaos. And this Ritz situation—everything around Ritz period—was a bit much for Randolph. He made himself unavailable to his parents for the time being.

Ritchie felt it was time to step up and put his family back together. Or, at the very least, it was time to face the consequences of his actions of thirty-plus years before.

He had to face his daughter, look in her eyes, and tell her the truth. She deserved to know why her father wasn't there for her. She deserved to know the whole story.

ABOUT THE AUTHORS

☆ ★ ☆

WENDY WILLIAMS, the self-proclaimed "Queen of All Media," is the host of the syndicated *The Wendy Williams Experience* (WBLS 107.5 FM in New York City), which airs weekdays in the coveted 2 P.M.–7 P.M. drive-time slot, and has been named "Radio Personality of the Year" by *Billboard*. She's no stranger to TV and is the author of the *New York Times* bestsellers *The Wendy Williams Experience* and *Wendy's Got the Heat*.

KAREN HUNTER is a Pulitzer Prize–winning journalist and former editorial board member of the New York *Daily News*. Hunter has coauthored several *New York Times* bestsellers, including *On the Down Low*, by J. L. King, and Wendy Williams's nonfiction books.